Dear Ellen Bee

Dear Ellen Bee

A CIVIL WAR SCRAPBOOK of TWO UNION SPIES

by MARY E. LYONS & MURIEL M. BRANCH

ATHENEUM BOOKS FOR YOUNG READERS
NEW YORK · LONDON · TORONTO · SYDNEY · SINGAPORE

Atheneum Books for Young Readers
An imprint of Simon & Schuster Children's Publishing Division
1230 Avenue of the Americas, New York, New York 10020

Book design by David Caplan
The text of this book is set in Fairfield LH and Bodoni Old Face.
Printed in the United States of America
4 6 8 10 9 7 5 3

Library of Congress Cataloging-in-Publication Data
Lyons, Mary E.
Dear Ellen Bee : a civil war scrapbook of two union spies /
by Mary E. Lyons, Muriel M. Branch.   p. cm.
Summary: A scrapbook kept by a young black girl details her experiences and those of the older
white woman, "Miss Bet," who had freed her and her family, sent her north from Richmond to get an
education, and then worked to bring an end to slavery. Based on the life of Elizabeth Van Lew.
ISBN 0-689-82379-7
1. Van Lew, Elizabeth L., 1818-1900—Juvenile fiction. [1. Van Lew, Elizabeth L.,
1818-1900—Fiction. 2. Slavery—Fiction. 3. Abolitionists—Fiction. 4. United States—History—
1849-1877—Fiction. 5. United States—History—Civil War, 1861-1865—
Fiction. 6. Scrapbooks—Fiction.] I. Branch, Muriel Miller. II. Title.
PZ7.L99556 E1 2000   [Fic]—dc21   99-42050

To Lauren Winner, who saved me in December
—M. E. L.

In honor of women
—M. M. B.

Prologue

Now begins my little book.
Lovely eyes on thee will look.

—FROM A NINETEENTH-CENTURY CHILD'S SCRAPBOOK

My dear niece, Polly Bowser,

When I was your age, I thought I was something special. And why wouldn't I, with everybody always telling me so? You know, too much attention can go right to a child's head.

Anyway, in those days every decent young lady had a scrapbook where she could store treasures and write secret thoughts. Being that I was so special, I figured Miss Bet should give me one, too, and of course I got my way. All sorts of things landed in the album. Letters, flowers, cards, sketches, diary entries . . . for a while, this messy book held my whole self between its covers.

That was over forty years ago.

I wish I had a feathered hat for every time I've opened it since then, hoping to find my long-ago times. But when I read about the dark days of the Civil War (I call them the hanging days), my fingers start to shake.

I guess memories can't make us young again, and this is how it should be. So you keep the book now, Polly. Maybe it'll be a friend to you the way it was to me. . . . Sometimes it felt like the only friend I had.

Inside are the thoughts of a scared young girl. You'll also see letters from Bet Van Lew (I saved even the dangerous ones) and my answers to her. I slipped these into the book when Miss Bet returned them years ago.

Along with the letters she gave me some sheets torn from her own album. Her words and mementos were too private, she said, for anyone's eyes but mine. Miss Bet wrote her deepest feelings in her scrapbook, and as you read her pages, Polly, you'll see she was no ordinary woman. It took courage to do what she did in Richmond during the Civil War.

Richmond, Virginia, was real contented with itself before

the war began. People were making money from flour mills, to-bacco factories, iron works, and slave trading. These folks lived on the city's highest hills, where it was easy to look down on workers below . . . German and Irish immigrants, poor whites, free Negroes, and hired-out slaves.

But Miss Bet wasn't contented at all about slavery. If only she'd stayed on her hill like the other rich white women! Things might have been different if she'd minded her own business. She lost everything, yet it never occurred to her to give up the fight.

You'll see, Polly, that my album pages are topped with a leaf and Miss Bet's with a vine. And I've put all the papers in order by date, so you'll have a story. Not just an ordinary tale about the Civil War, which freed our people from slavery. Most folks think rifles and cannons put down the Southern rebellion.

No, this scrapbook tells of Ellen Bee, two spies who won the war with softer weapons . . . a bowl of custard, a faded bonnet, a loaf of bread, and an old leather shoe.

LOVE,

AUNT LIZA

1856–1860

Presented
to
Liza
by her
Miss Bet
1856

Liza, you insisted on a scrapbook for your birthday, so here it is, my dear. Please use the album as I have used mine—as a literary pocketbook and an occasional journal. Years from now it will bring back memories of your long, useful life.

And a free life it shall be! Tucked behind this page is a second gift—the beginning of my grand plan for your future. Carry the emancipation paper with you at all times. If patrollers try to sell you back into slavery, you will need proof of your free status. This is important, now that you will be traveling.

Your third gift is money for a train ticket to Philadelphia. You will leave at the end of May, as I want you to learn the city well over the summer.

In September, you will begin the preparatory program at the Quaker School for Free Negroes. At age thirteen, you will begin their high school, and at fifteen, the Normal School curriculum. I have arranged for you to stay with Widow Robert, who runs a boardinghouse nearby.

Though I am sure Nelson and Caroline will miss their little girl, your parents know I mean to secure a good life for you, and I do believe you will make a splendid teacher one day! With every good wish for your birthday, I remain

Miss Bet

State of Virginia

City of Richmond, to wit:

Mary Liza Van Lew a *child* of color, has this day applied for a certificate in the Clerk's Office of the Hustings Court, which is granted *her* ; and *she* is now of the following description, to wit: *4* feet 5½ inches high, of a *Chocolate* complexion, has *wide-set eyes, keen features strong teeth, no scars, tall for her years, can read and write. Said child is emancipated in the court this day by Mrs. Van Lew. She will be residing in Pennsylvania to return to the Commonwealth in the summer months, permission granted by an order of this court.*

In Testimony whereof, I, Robert Howard, Clerk of the said Hustings Court, have hereto set my hand and affixed the Seal of the said court, this *16th* day of *May* A.D., 1856

Ro. Howard

MAY 18, 1856

This is the most beautifullest book in the world, but Miss Bet can keep her old money. Philadelphia! Never seen it and don't want to. She's treating me like I'm a baby. Well, I'm *not* her baby! I won't go. Not now, not ever!

MAY 25, 1856

10 A.M.

Dear Lord, if You're everywhere like my mama says You are, then You just have to look out for poor Liza in this Negro car today. It's hotter than Mama's oven. Cinders keep blowing in the window and peppering my hands. I have to blow them off this page as I write, and the yellow dress Mama made for me is already looking like mustard.

Miss Bet says Philadelphia is a pretty city. I don't believe her. She says, "Liza, a young lady needs the higher branches of learning to finish her education." Well, here's what I say.

I liked things the way they were in Richmond, with Miss Bet teaching me to read and write. I liked sitting at the tall desk in her library, copying drawings from her Mr. Shake A. Spear books. Anyhow, what would I do with that higher branch she's talking about? She knows Mama won't let me climb trees.

Oh, Mama! She wouldn't even come to the station this morning. She woke Daddy and me before daybreak, and we all huddled around the kitchen table. I guess she'd been up awhile, because she'd already packed me a basket of cold chicken, boiled eggs, and custard.

Mama's face was torn up from crying. Seeing her like that made me cry, too. She covered my hands with hers.

"Well, baby," Mama said, "I thought our separating days was over four years ago, back when Miz Van Lew bought you and me from old man Lorton so we could live here with your daddy. Thought she sure enough wanted us to be a family."

Daddy poured coffee from his cup into the saucer, like he always does when he's upset. He says drinking it this way slows down his thoughts so he can hear them. "Now Caroline," he corrected. "You know this ain't the same."

"How come?" I asked.

Daddy took a long, serious slurp from the saucer. "'Cause Miss Bet ain't selling you off to some slaveholder in the Deep South. That's slavery separation. Miss Bet got a good heart. She's the one that pestered her mama to free us, remember?"

Daddy's so sensible sometimes, he just wears me out. And I'm plenty tired of him always siding with Miss Bet.

"If we're so free," I begged, "then tell her I can't go. What if I don't want to be a teacher? Maybe I'd rather be an artist, instead!"

"Teacher, free, slave," Mama said. "What's the difference? Separating is separating, and it don't pain my heart no less." Then she started plaiting my hair, crying all the while.

I miss Mama. Feels like her tears are still woven into my braids. And I'll never understand that Miss Bet. First she fixed it so Mama and I could live with Daddy in the Van Lew kitchen house. Then she sends me away. Does she bother to ask us what we want? No, she goes right ahead and makes her plans, exactly like she always does.

2 P.M.

We just stopped at the Fredericksburg depot. Some colored boys came through selling biscuits and apples, until a lard-bellied white man made them get off. I guess he's one of those slave catchers Miss Bet warned me about. He ordered everybody to show their papers and passes.

I couldn't find mine anywhere! My hands shook so bad, I dropped this album on the floor. I picked it up and pressed the only piece of home I had to my chest.

"What's this book you got here, gal?" he said.

"Just a scrapbook, massa." Didn't want to call him massa, 'cause I'm a free girl now, but I was scared not to.

When he snatched it from me, my freedom paper fell out. He squinted at it for a while, and that's when I noticed the words were upside down. Great big bully couldn't even read. I felt like giggling, till he shoved it back in my book like a piece of trash. Then he threw the book at me like I was trash, too.

I'm going to save this ticket stub forever, so I never forget what Miss Bet's done to me!

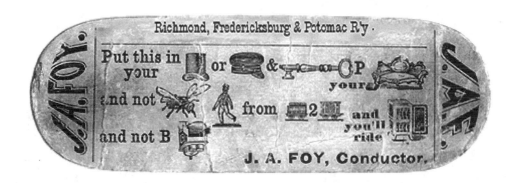

MAY 25, 1856
6 P.M.

Nelson drove Liza and me to the Main Street station at dawn. She accepted my good-bye embrace, though it was Nelson who received the buttercups—she tossed a bouquet to him as the car pulled from the station.

We came back to a house in mourning.

"Oh, my goodness gracious so," Mother said, sighing at the dining room table. "The mansion is too quiet. . . . Did Liza seem upset?"

"The child will be fine, Mother," I assured her. "After all, you sent me away to school in Philadelphia, and I survived."

"You were fifteen, Miss Bet," Caroline said, sniffling. "Liza's only ten!" She slapped a platter of biscuits on the table.

"I wish you had come with us, Caroline," I replied. "A farewell kiss from you might have cheered Liza a bit."

"My girl and I said our good-byes in private." I could barely hear her words, but the tearful tone was clear enough. "You know Liza's my only baby," she added.

Well, she is my only child, too, I thought. Of course, I would never say the words aloud. I remember the first time Nelson placed Liza in my arms. What a pair of odorous surprises that angel baby produced, and right on the sleeves of my new morning dress. But from then on, my heart belonged to her. No one will miss her more than I will.

How could I explain my feelings to anyone in the house? They must never know I love Liza as if she were my own . . . the child I may never have with A. T. Well, enough of this! She must complete her schooling. I will not have my girl waiting on spoiled white women.

27 Chestnut Street

Philadelphia, Pennsylvania

June 15, 1856

Dear Miss Bet,

    The pen and ink must be scarce that you don't write. If you knew how much I missed home, you'd write me every day. I don't like Philadelphia. The people chop up their words and spit them out too fast. And they have bad manners. Daddy always says good manners don't cost a cent.

    Only thing that makes me feel better is drawing. I made a picture of my Sabbath School teacher. Tell Mama and Daddy hello.

Liza

2311 E. Grace Street

Richmond, Virginia

June 20, 1856

Dear Liza,

    Remember, every grown-up was young once. Though I am past thirty now, I still recall my first week at The Philadelphia Academy for Young Ladies. The nights were so lonely. How I longed to be in the library at home—to rest my head on Mother's shoulder while Papa read to Brother and me.

    Yes, the rude Northern tongues shocked me, too, and I sorely

7

missed my Virginia friends, especially . . . well, just know that everything you feel, I have felt before.

Perhaps these new frocks will cheer you. Today I chose two designs from Godey's Lady's Book, and Mother thinks a nice blue poplin and a brown merino would suit you well. After all, as a member of the Van Lew household, you should try to look your best. I will send the dresses as soon as Caroline stitches them up. Meanwhile, I am enclosing the picture so you will have something to look forward to.

Caroline says to tell you the two runt kittens you named "Ugly" and "Not So" are sleeping in your bed. She also reminds you to wash behind your ears every morning.

MISS BET

JUNE 21, 1856

This letter from A. T. delivered by Brother. "When I left Overton Plantation this morning," John said, "your beau's eyes were red and swollen. The man's all to pieces, Bet."

> *June 21, 1856*
> *Overton Plantation*
> *Goochland County, Virginia*

Dear Fiancée,

Are you out of your lovely head? You haven't written in weeks, and now I know why.

Yesterday your brother rode out to buy a load of lumber. I invited him for dinner and to stay the night, and midway through the pork chops I inquired after y'all's mother. John stared at his wine goblet for the longest time. He's a kind fellow, Bet. He knew the news would break me.

"Mother freed our slaves last month," he finally admitted. "Most have stayed on as paid servants . . . Nelson and Caroline as cook and gardener, James as handyman, Mary to clean. Bob and Oliver will still work the Van Lew farm. The rest are employed at our hardware stores."

The rice and gravy turned to paste in my throat. "Good God, man! You can't run five stores without slaves. That's why your father left no provisions in his will to free them."

John nodded. "Mother and Bet have discussed the slaves since father died in forty-three. Mother's past sixty and fragile now. I think Sister finally wore her down."

How well I know your power to charm and cajole, Bet. I

reminded John that the stores have made a small fortune for your family, and asked him if he wanted to throw away the profits on paid labor. He defended you with great feeling.

"Bet's the oldest," he said. "It's she who's carried all the family responsibilities since our father died, and I should respect her decisions."

John is too loyal to criticize his sister, but someone must speak for him. How will he pay for the new porticoed house he's bought for his wife and two-year-old daughter? And your mother . . . she raised you and John in the grandest mansion on the highest hill in Richmond. Virginia's finest families have eaten at the Van Lew table, including the Lees and the Cabells. What of her high social standing with them?

What's worse, John says you've sent your little Negro girl to Philadelphia. I should have known. Isn't that where you met those meddlesome abolitionists? Watch her carefully when she returns! Learning makes a Negro unfit for service—think of Nat Turner and his murderous gang of runaways.

Bet, you waste great affection on your coloreds but leave me hanging like a ham in the smokehouse. I've explained time and again that every great civilization was built on the backs of slaves. Yet for years you've refused to set a wedding date because I won't free my servants.

For too long you've kept me chained as a bachelor. Now I fear you'll be a spinster forever. Life will be empty without my Bet's brilliant eyes and impossible blond hair, but I cannot, I will not, marry an abolitionist. Please keep the watch I gave you the night we were engaged. May it remind you of sweeter times. John is loading the wagon, so I must quickly close.

WITH DEEP REGRET,

A. T.

Oh, A. T., my heart's love! I shall write him tomorrow, after my own tears have stopped. Write to say I have wept, too, but not just for us. If he were here with me, he could hear a mournful sound pouring through the window. It is the singing of slaves in the stifling tobacco factories down on the James River.

Slaves are songbirds of sorrow, yet he never listens. Southern custom has deadened his senses, and he remembers only the history that suits him. Those great civilizations—Egypt, Greece, Rome—were built on rotten foundations. They crumbled, as will the South one day.

I have always known right from wrong, now more than ever. But Sweet Jesus, I feel so alone. First Liza, now A. T. . . . both gone!

27 CHESTNUT STREET

PHILADELPHIA, PENNSYLVANIA

JULY 15, 1856

Dear Miss Bet,

I haven't had one chance to write y'all again. Between sweeping Widow Robert's parlor every afternoon and going to Sabbath School, these Philadelphia folks are taking up all my time.

Miss Bet, this house is so gloomy. It reminds me of your cobwebby wine cellar. And the Widow is hard to describe. She's a busty woman, with skinny legs. Sort of like a tadpole with a bun on top. I don't think she likes me.

Something bad happened today. I've been storing my trunk in a corner of my room to keep it out of the way, but she found it.

"What's all this?" she asked. Then she poked through my private things—even my drawers and shifts! "Well, now, aren't you the lazy one?"

"No, m'am, I'm not!" I told her. "I just don't plan to stay around here too long. I figure I need clean clothes for the trip back home."

"Liza, you should be grateful that Bet Van Lew has given you the gift of an education. Unpack before dinner, or I'll twist your ears."

Miss Bet, the words fell out of her mouth faster than pulled teeth, so I didn't have a chance to say anything before she swished out of the room. And what does it mean to twist somebody's ears? Is that why Mama says to keep them clean?

The other girls who board here are friendly, especially my room-mate, Sarah. They've signed the calling cards I drew in my album, and they try to make me talk, but I've been too miserable. Got nothing to say. Besides, they're here because they want to be. You might as well hold on to those dresses, Miss Bet. I've decided to come home.

LIZA

RULES
OF THE
SABBATH SCHOOL.

Every Scholar in this School must agree to the following Rules :

1. I must always mind the Superintendant and ALL the Teachers of this School.
2. I must come every Sunday, and be here when School goes in.
3. I must go to my seat as soon as I come in.
4. I MUST ALWAYS BE STILL.
5. I must not leave my seat till School is through.
6. I must take good care of my books.
7. I must not LEAN on the next scholar.
8. I must walk SOFTLY in the School.
9. I must learn all my lessons well, and be ready to say them when called upon by my Teacher.
10. I must not make a noise by the Church door, or School door, but must go in as soon as I come there.
11. I must always go to Church.
12. I must behave well in the street when I am going to Church.
13. I must walk softly into Church.
14. I must sit still in my place till Church goes out.
15. I must go away from the Church as soon as I go out.

P.S. Philadelphia is a strict place. I'm sending a list of rules so you'll know how awful it is. For six weeks I've tried to obey them all, but Miss Bet, number four is the hardest, meanest rule in the world.

2311 E. Grace Street
Richmond, Virginia
July 31, 1856

Dear Liza,

I declare, my patience is gone. No child ever died from sitting still in church. Instead of complaining, say a prayer of thanks. You have always been allowed to worship in a pew, both here at St. John's and now in Philadelphia. Think of the sad-faced slaves who attend St. John's. Most climb a ladder and crowd into the balcony over the door. Remember how you called it the chicken roost because it was so narrow?

Fill each day with useful activities, and the rest of 1856 will pass quickly enough. Begin by reading all you can. Remember, the Van Lews are an intellectual family, and you were weaned on books in Papa's library.

I recommend Frederick Douglass's narratives and William Garrison's abolitionist newspaper, The Liberator. Study their ideas on ending slavery, for the holy flames of abolition will destroy slavery one day. Education will prepare you to do your part.

Mother misses the sound of your feet running through the halls and has embroidered a bookmark to aid you when school begins. May it also help you accept your responsibilities, as I have accepted mine.

Miss Bet

JULY 31, 1856

James just left to post my stern letter to Liza, but who am I to tell her to pray? Lately I cannot find God anywhere, even in church. Every Sunday morning I watch the people enter St. John's across the way—slaveholding Episcopalians who nod and smile and feel blessed.

And why shouldn't they? The minister himself approves of their wickedness. Mother needs me to return the marble stares we've received since freeing the slaves, otherwise, I would never go to church at all.

Today I must file store receipts and plan the week's menus. Am riding out to the farm tomorrow to confer with Oliver. He says the tobacco barn needs a new roof. So much to do! Still, I welcome the distractions, as they leave little time for missing my girl or A. T. . . . .

2311 E. GRACE STREET
RICHMOND, VIRGINIA
DECEMBER 13, 1856

Dear Liza,

Enclosed is an early Christmas gift—money for a round-trip ticket to Richmond. Your parents say they long for their Liza, and Mother agrees, so you will be here for two weeks.

The mansion and the kitchen house already smell like Christmas. Nelson has draped running cedar over the doors, just as he always does, and Mary is shelling mounds of walnuts for your mother's pound cakes.

James is at the farm today to dig a roasting pit for his family reunion on the big day. You know that scores of his kin are still enslaved on nearby plantations, and Christmas is the only time when masters will let them travel. How I wish we could buy and free them all! Anyway, he says, "Tell Liza to count on eating lots of pig."

So, my dear, we are all anxious to see our girl and give her many merry kisses.

MUCH AFFECTION,

MISS BET

Ah, the gifts of summer! Raspberries and cream for breakfast. Skeins of clouds at sunset, streaked purple and orange. And my lovely Liza all day long, every day until school starts again in August—without a sign of the complaints that filled her letters last year.

Mary muttered about the noise when she brought breakfast to my chamber this morning. "I declare, Miss Bet, if that child slams the veranda door one more time, I'm going to make James take it off."

"An empty threat, Mary." I tried not to smile. "You would have to kill flies all day."

"Huh. Chase them flies into a spare bedroom, close the door, and charge 'em rent."

My heart was too light to argue, though Mary is right. When I looked out the window, there was Liza, flitting from the kitchen house to the mansion. Then, wham!

The library seems to be her favorite spot these days. She has been devouring Papa's books one by one—has even counted them. "Five hundred and seventy-seven, Miss Bet," she said. She claims she would read them all by year's end if she didn't have to go back to school. Well, my girl *will* go back, and one day thank me for it.

27 CHESTNUT STREET

PHILADELPHIA, PENNSYLVANIA

SEPTEMBER 8, 1857

Dear Miss Bet,

Do you remember last Christmas, when you sent me back for

more suffering? I've been throwing up again, just like I did then. Miss Bet, two months in the summer with Mama and Daddy isn't enough! I should be used to it by now, since this is my second year in school. But the onliest thing that happens is I get homesick all over again.

So I got out my album, and I've been sitting on the Widow's front porch, drawing pictures and trying to cheer myself up. I came across one of last year's letters with a bookmark in it. THY WILL BE DONE, it says. I hate to tell you, Miss Bet, but I never once used that bookmark. It mixed me up. Whose will you talking about? Yours or God's?

You're always telling me I'd make a good teacher and abolitionist. Well, what if I want to be an artist instead? And why can't I come home to finish my higher branches with you? It's hot enough in my school building to make light bread rise, and I live with the meanest woman in the city. A widow! I bet she's got her husband buried somewhere in the yard.

Just this morning at breakfast, she said I probably wouldn't amount to much, since I was born in the South. The other girls giggled, except Sarah. She's from Georgia, and I don't think Tadpole likes her, either.

On top of this, Mrs. Douglas, my history teacher, wanted to take us students to an abolitionist meeting at the Banneker Institute. The speaker was going to tell us about the Dred Scott decision. About how that poor man thought he could walk away from slavery when he traveled to a free state with his master. Can you believe it, Miss Bet? My teacher says the Supreme Court ruled that even in a free state, a slave is still a slave!

Well, anyway, we were all fixed to ride one of the new horse cars, but the conductor wouldn't accept our nickels. "Negroes not allowed on this line!" he hollered. Then he shooed us down the steps of the car like we were mangy cats. Miss Bet, one time you said everything I feel, you have felt before. Well, I don't think so. I bet nobody ever made you feel as low down as that white man did me that day. I know I'm here to get an education, but I'm learning some things I'd soon not know.

LIZA

P.S. See how well I can draw?

OCTOBER 1857

Please, God, let Miss Bet's copy get lost in the mail.

May 17, 1858

My twelfth birthday, but nobody in the house except Sarah breathed one mumbling word. At least she gave me a hug and a sketch pad. If Daddy saw her, he'd say she looks like his fishing pole, she's so straight up and down, but Sarah's sweet. When she smiles, her dimples cave in, and her eyes smile, too.

I wish I could be quiet like Sarah. She thinks I should do something about my bad conduct in school, especially talking. Says she'll give me her two best pencils if I try. I said, "Sarah, I can't help it, something just gets into me." I didn't tell her Miss Bet will give me all the pencils I want when I go home for the summer. Only three more weeks!

July 5, 1858

5:30 P.M.

An irritating afternoon. I took Liza to see the funeral procession for President Monroe's body. After twenty-seven years in a New York cemetery, he has returned home to rest in a marble tomb at Hollywood Cemetery. The casket was brought by steamer, and it seemed that most of Richmond's thirty-five thousand citizens came out to watch the arrival.

I tried to hold Liza's hand as we moved through the crowd, but she shook it off. I suppose my girl is too old for that now. All the same, it hurts my heart, and I feel that she is slipping away from me.

She was respectfully silent when the six white horses pulling the hearse passed by, but as we walked back home, the questions began.

"Miss Bet, wasn't President Monroe one of America's first patriots?"

"Quite so. He fought in the Revolution, was governor of Virginia twice, and twice president. . . . Liza, I am pleased to hear you use a word like 'patriot.'"

"History teacher taught me. Did Monroe own slaves?"

I wondered where these questions were going. "Yes, my dear, Monroe held slaves."

"Then why are you celebrating?"

Good Lord, I thought, this child should be an attorney, not a teacher.

"It is true, Liza, that slavery was a troublesome issue for the statesmen who set up our government. Some, like George Washington, continued to hold slaves, though he left them free in his will. James Monroe, I believe, did not free his slaves during his lifetime or after his death."

We slowed our steps as we began the steep climb up Church Hill.

Liza took off her straw bonnet and dabbed her upper lip with a hankie, and oh, how I wished for a glass of Caroline's lemonade!

"Put your hat back on, dear, or the sun will give you a headache. There is no excuse for it, but I am afraid our country's first leaders took the easy way out. The Constitution does not make slavery legal, but it does not make it illegal, either. Still, anyone who fought in the Revolution is a hero to me. Without soldiers like Monroe, we would still be ruled by an English king."

"Miss Bet," Liza whined, "don't be like Monroe. Don't make me go back to school in August."

What in the world? I thought. Does she think I treat her like a slave? She knows I do not! This is simply a ploy to get her own way.

We rested for a moment in the shade of Mrs. Carrington's maple tree, and I tried to distract my scheming child.

"Enjoy July and August, Liza. By September, you will be ready to see your friends and teachers again. And ready to study hard, too."

Bah! The girl is so annoying sometimes. She said not another word, and when we reached the mansion, she cut through the side yard and ran straight to the kitchen house.

What can I do? She is in a perfect snit, but I have no time to fix it—I must dress for the banquet in honor of Monroe. Well, I shall tell Caroline to remind Liza to look in the night sky. The Capitol building will be lit up—perhaps the glow will lighten her mood. I hope so, for tomorrow we are having a *serious* discussion about her school marks.

SEPTEMBER 1, 1858

Back in Philadelphia for another year with Tadpole. Miss Bet said the meanest thing when she put me on the train. Said if I don't do better in school, she might send me to the colored Charity School. She says I'd have to take classes for four hours a day, and cook and wash and sew and mend for another eight. I think she's bluffing!

Books I have to read for fall term:

The English Reader: or Pieces in Prose and Poetry, Selected from the Best Writers. Designed to Assist Young Persons to Read With Propriety and Effect: to Improve Their Language and Sentiments, and to Inculcate Some of the Most Important Principles of Piety and Virtue. With a Few Preliminary Observations on the Principles of Good Reading.

Aids to English Composition, Prepared for Students of All Grades

A Book of Common School History

A System of Questions in Geography

English Grammar, Made Easy to the Teacher and Pupil

Elements of Algebra

27 CHESTNUT STREET
PHILADELPHIA, PENNSYLVANIA
SEPTEMBER 5, 1858

Dear Miss Bet,

Guess what? Sarah's sponsor let her come back for another year, and the Widow put us in the same room again. Today Sarah showed me how to make paper dolls from advertisements and mount them on cardboard. We're teaching the dolls how to do algebra, but they're not too good at it yet.

I've been working hard on my conduct and my lessons, Miss Bet. The history teacher gave me her old copies of The Liberator—I'm sending you one to prove I've been reading them—and she took me to an abolitionist meeting last Wednesday evening. I learned a lot from the speakers, especially the former slave. Mama and Daddy and I were slaves, but at least you never beat us until our bodies got all whelped up.

A free Negro man spoke, too. Miss Bet, do you know how bad your "City of Brotherly Love" treats free coloreds? The Irish and Germans have pushed Negro men out of all the decent factory jobs. And Negroes can't sit in the same orchestra seats as white people. Can't go to church with whites, either. Only Catholics and Quakers let them in.

Miss Bet, I don't think I want to be an abolitionist. I'd have to speak at a meeting, and that would make me too nervous. What if I wet my drawers? Daddy always says, "If you don't stand for something, you'll fall flat on your face," but I don't think I'm going to join this slavery fight.

LOVE,

LIZA

2311 E. Grace Street
Richmond, Virginia
October 15, 1858

Dear Liza,

You are my star child! Six weeks of school and already a Certificate of Achievement in history. And a blue ribbon in art class. I wish I could have seen the head mistress present them.

You will be a head mistress yourself one day, Liza, for this is the next step in my plan for you. After you become a teacher, I shall set up a small academy for free children here on Church Hill. All books and supplies will be provided, and you can live here in the mansion with me.

Caroline made lemonade and chocolate pie for your father's birthday. The weather is too cool at last for mosquitoes, so this afternoon on the veranda we drank to his health and toasted his genius daughter. Your parents say a twelve-year-old is not too old for twenty hugs and fifty kisses. I send these, along with congratulations from your own

Miss Bet

NOVEMBER 12, 1858

Oh, dear Lord, how will I live through my third year of school? Sarah got a letter today with a Georgia postmark. It was from the daughter of the old lady who freed her. Sarah and I read it together on the front steps.

"'Dear Sarah,'" my friend began, "'this letter is to inform you that my mother died last week.'" When Sarah started to cry, I held her hand and finished the hateful words:

"'I regret that you must return to Macon immediately. Mother's debts are many, and the family can no longer afford to educate a Negro girl.'"

So I'm losing the only friend I've got in Philadelphia. I feel bad I get to stay in school, when Sarah's the one who wants to be a teacher, not me. I made her sign my album tonight because she's taking the train at dawn to-morrow.

> To Liza
> Oft in tender recollection
> Call to mind your absent friend
> Cherish for her that affection
> Which she hopes will never end.
> Your friend and schoolmate,
> Sarah Murdoch

RICHMOND, VIRGINIA

DECEMBER 25, 1858

Woke up with a Christmas present I don't want—cramps in my stomach and blood on the sheets. When Mama found me curled up in bed, she said, "Liza, you look like a twist of chewing tobacco. Didn't I warn you about eating those three slices of sweet potato pie last . . ."

So I told her I thought I'd started my monthlies. Right away Mama threw on a shawl and went downstairs. She came back with rags and a jar of hot water wrapped in a towel. Said the warmth would ease the binding in my belly.

"Put these in your drawers and wash them out at night," she said, handing me the rags. Her voice quivered, like that first morning when I left for Philadelphia. "You're a young woman now. I can't call you my baby anymore."

I wish she hadn't said that. Suppose I don't want to be a woman just yet? I can't get used to the idea—going to bed a girl and waking up a woman. It's scary.

APRIL 1859

This should prove to Miss Bet I'm smart enough. When I go home for the summer, I'm staying for good!

THE TEACHER'S CERTIFICATE.

Miss *Mary Liza Van Lew* a member of Class No. *6th* in *the Quaker School for Free Negroes* is awarded this **CERTIFICATE**, as a Token of Approbation for acquirements and standing—for the *Term* ending *October 7th 1858* 18*8*

Time is more precious than gold.	The choicest of all treasures, Which human search can find, Are those uncloying pleasures Which centre in the mind. — Reason should always guide, And o'er our acts preside. — Delight in what you undertake to learn.	" Just as the twig is bent, the tree's inclined."
ATTENDANCES.	**RECITATIONS.**	**DEPORTMENT.**
Early Attendances . . . . . . *24* Late do. . . . . *1* Total do. *25*	Amount required . . . . *80* Amount given . . . . *79* Deficiency *1*	Correct, represented by No. . . . . . . *18* Deduct for misconduct . . . . *2* Grade of Scholarship . . . . . *A*
By idleness and play, Some squander time away.	" Youth is the time for the progress in all arts : Then use your youth to gain the noblest parts.	*Mildred Douglas* Instructer

2311 E. Grace Street
Richmond, Virginia
May 1859

Dear Liza,
    I am afraid that a summer visit will be impossible this year.

Richmond officials have recently passed a hideous set of rules for slaves and free Negroes.

It appears that nothing will slow this flood of hate. First, the Fugitive Slave Act of 1850 . . . no free state is free, not when a slave who reaches its border can be recaptured by the slaveholder. Then the Dred Scott decision two years ago. And now this.

Read the rules carefully, my dear, and pray for the safety of Richmond's colored citizens. Most offenses are punishable with thirty-nine stripes. Number twenty-seven would be comical if it weren't so cruel. If a white person unlawfully beats a slave, he may be fined an entire dollar!

An Ordinance Concerning Negroes

1. Who are deemed negroes.
2. Slave absent from home, how punished.
3. What pass to designate, who to give it, when to be endorsed.
4. When fine may be instead of stripes.
5. Persons signing or endorsing pass without authority, how punished.
6. When slaves not to ride in hack or carriage.
7. What places negroes not to walk in.
8. Where negroes not to smoke.
9. Negro not to keep a cook-shop or eating house.
10. Negro not to carry a cane at night.
11. Negroes not to stand or pass on sidewalks.
12. Not to organize secret societies or attend them.
13. Slave not to rent room or house.
14. Slave not to hire himself out or board himself. Owner or hirer to provide him with board, and give list of slaves boarded to mayor.
15. Free negro not to permit slave to remain on his lot.
16. Not to sell ardent spirits to slaves.
17. Free negroes to have copy of free papers.

18. *Not to be employed without copy of free papers.*
19. *Slave not to be hired without consent of master.*
20. *Negro to be punished for provoking language, gestures, or indecent exposure.*
21. *White person not to give or sell weapons to negro. Negro not to keep them.*
22. *Not to sell medicine to slave. Slave or free negro not to administer medicine.*
23. *Negro engaging in riot, etc., or committing a trespass, how punished.*
24. *What is an unlawful assembly of negroes around churches.*
25. *What is an unlawful assembly of negroes upon lot.*
26. *How negroes in such assembly arrested and punished. Person allowing such assembly fined.*
27. *Persons beating slaves, how punished.*

Land's sake—too excited to sleep! I walked all by myself to the Library Company for an abolitionist lecture. The Widow said I could, since I'm thirteen now and got good school marks in the spring. Only I was a sweaty mess when I got there, so I sat in the back.

That's when I saw *HIM*, standing in the corner. Looking at *ME!* I stared back, but only for a second. Didn't take too long to notice those jet-black eyes and smooth skin. And he dresses so manly. Nothing at all like the acorn-brain boys in my school. Long black frock coat, necktie, and a starched collar as sharp as shears.

I couldn't believe it when the president of the Young Man's Abolition Society introduced HIM as the speaker . . . Wilson Bowser, a sixteen-year-old *honor* student from the Institute for Colored Youth.

When Wilson spoke, his voice cracked every now and then, but mostly it was deep, like the washtub bass the colored men play down by the river in Richmond. He kept looking my way, and I got so flustered, I missed most of the speech until the end.

"Finally, ladies and gentleman," he said, "beware of those people who are offering to load us Negroes on a ship for a one-way trip back to Africa."

Wilson grabbed the lectern hard enough to lift it off the floor. "We don't want a colony in Liberia. We want to ride the streetcars in Philadelphia, to go to schools and churches of our choice, and to vote. Let them know we will speak up and out until every Negro is granted the same rights as the white man!"

Sounded to me like Wilson Bowser could end discrimination all by himself if he'd a mind to. I wanted to steal some more glances at him, but Mama always says don't let the dark catch you out. Soon as it was polite to leave, I walked downstairs to the door. Then he caught up with me and TOUCHED MY ELBOW!

"May I walk you home, miss?" he said. "It's getting late."

I could have fainted! Only time a boy's ever talked to me is when I played marbles with colored children in Richmond, and I don't guess that counts as talking.

On the way back to the Widow's house, we yakked about Richmond's "Ordinance Concerning Negroes" (he says the laws are an abomination) and Shakespeare's plays, and desserts (his favorite is bread pudding, but I told him I never learned to cook), and the best way to clean metal (lemon juice and salt), and just about everything. He even signed my album.

Best of all, Wilson is a Richmond boy. His daddy runs a barber shop on Second Street, and his Mama is a seamstress. She's friends with a woman who knows a woman who knows my mama. So he's practically family!

I heard Moses speak tonight. That's what I told Wilson when we left National Hall. I bet Moses even looked like Frederick Douglass. Must have, because Douglass's face seems to be carved out of stone, and I think he could stare at God without blinking once.

Miss Bet's always said Mr. Douglass was a powerful-talking man, and she's right. His mama was hired out by a slaveholder when he was just a babe. He never even knew her. After he was separated from his grandmammy at age seven, he was sent to another plantation. At sixteen, after two tries and some kicking and punching, he finally escaped to Baltimore, Maryland.

But Wilson thinks Miss Bet forgot to tell me some things about Mr. Douglass. He says I need to know more about the abolitionists who made Douglass famous, especially William Lloyd Garrison. So this morning Wilson brought over Mr. Douglass's autobiography *My Bondage and My Freedom*. I've been reading it for hours, and I'm so mad!

Why would Garrison and his Anti-Slavery Society make Mr. Douglass famous, then stop giving money to his *North Star* paper? You'd think they would have helped him, just like they do other abolitionist papers.

But Mr. Garrison thinks preaching and stamping his foot is the only way to end slavery, while Mr. Douglass believes politics and new laws are the answer. So Douglass has run his own *Frederick Douglass's Weekly* for fourteen years, mostly by himself.

Garrisonians believe in ending slavery. My question is, why don't they believe we can think for ourselves once we're free?

NATIONAL HALL!

FRED'K DOUGLASS

Will LECTURE before the
ALUMNI ASSOCIATION

Of the INSTITUTE FOR COLORED YOUTHS,
Friday Eve'g, April 24,
AT NATIONAL HALL!

SUBJECT: AFFAIRS OF THE
NATION!

TICKETS 25 CENTS.

They may be had at J. E. GOULD'S MUSIC STORE, 632 Chestnut Street, and also
at the Office of the Lebanon Cemetery, 717 Lombard Street.

Doors open at 7.1-2 oclock.   Lecture to commence at 8.

RINGWALT & BROWN, Steam-Power Printers, 111 & 113 South Fourth St.

WHITE SULPHUR SPRINGS, VIRGINIA

AUGUST 10, 1859

8 P.M.

Slept like a top after an exhausting stagecoach ride over the Alleghenies. Mother and I were out-of-sorts when we arrived. Two thousand people have come to take the waters, including some Richmonders who still clip us for what they call our "Negroism."

Yesterday morning in the dining hall, Mrs. Cabell and Mrs. Randolph sailed right by us. They nodded briefly—I suppose they are still too respectful of the Van Lew name and wealth to ignore us entirely. Mother gave them both a gracious smile, but a moment later her face fell, and she quietly laid down her fork. "Why do they keep hurting us so?" she asked. "Mrs. Cabell and I used to be so close. She was the first to receive an invitation to hear Edgar Allan Poe read his poetry in our drawing room. And do you remember when Jenny Lind sang at our charity gala?"

I nodded. How well I remember the cream of society in our garden that day, sipping punch and eating Caroline's pastries. Everyone loved the soaring soprano voice of "the Swedish Nightingale," especially Mrs. Randolph, who covered Mother with pearly compliments.

"It's clear they like our money and our mansion," Mother said. Her voice slipped, then, like a piano string gone out of tune. "Yet for all that, they don't truly care about us."

The past three years have been hard on Mother, I know. Every cold look stings her pride, and I could kick these slaveholders to the curb for cutting her.

Mother feeling more content today. After breakfast, she purchased a sketch of Lover's Leap in the hotel store, pleased she could give me something for my album.

This afternoon she paddled in the spring with other guests. They all swear the sulphuric water cures bony pains, but the smell turns my stomach. I can almost taste it, as if a thousand matches were extinguished at once.

I begged to be excused, for the truth is, I would rather walk alone. How I love the lonely freedom of these hills! There's no one to sniff about abolition, or to make sly remarks about A. T. Mother's sketch brought back memories, so I took the path around Lover's Lane and strolled up to the Leap.

When a breeze stirred the pines, whispers floated through my head, calling me back to my first summer at the White—my thirteenth year—the summer I met Fannie. It all seems so long ago.

Dear girl . . . she's been dead for twenty years, but her words have haunted me since. When she told me her secret that clear August morning, I didn't understand the shame of it. What difference if her father earned his fortune by trading in human flesh? I can hear my silly reply now—

"Slavery is ordained by God," I assured her. "I have heard it said many times from St. John's pulpit in Richmond."

"But where did the Van Lew slaves come from?" she asked, and I was most ashamed that I did not know.

It had never crossed my mind that sometime, somewhere, the people we called "servants" had been bought and sold, too.

I remember how sick I felt when Fannie told me of the oozing wounds she once saw on the back of a Negro boy—a daring lad who had tried to run away from her father's slave pen just before an auction.

If only I had forgotten the vow Fannie made that day. As she looked out over the valley below, she swore she would never take a penny of her father's money after turning eighteen.

"Why, Fannie? Your father's sins are not yours!"

Her voice was firm. "Because, Bet, it is the right thing to do."

The right thing to do. At age fifteen, the words were simple and light. At forty-one, they feel like stones. God forgive me, I wish I had never met Fannie, for I might never have urged Mother to free our slaves. Now there are few parlors in Richmond where we can take our ease. Why must the path to goodness be a friendless one?

I wish I had not met A. T., either, but looking back, I suppose no thirteen-year-old girl could resist such a handsome older boy. The loops of brown curls, the teasing smile, those soft blue eyes! Any girl could drown looking into them. . . .

I miss Liza dreadfully. Be honest, Bet. As the sun tumbled behind the hills this evening, you missed A. T., too.

More plain food in the dining hall tonight. Mother adores the rustic bread and strong coffee, but wonders if Cook can make any dessert other than blackberry pie.

Dear Liza,

Received your letter Friday last. I am glad to hear you enjoyed July and August in Philadelphia and are looking forward to high school. Whatever has changed your mind about the city?

Mother is happy to be home from White Sulphur Springs. I wanted to stay another week, but she longed to see John's little Eliza, and I must admit that so much free time made me dwell too often on the past.

Your father has finished carving the weather vane he worked on all summer, and it is now installed on the roof. Not a sign of motion yet. The weather has been so hot and still that your mother calls it "Lazy Jack," though it is meant to be the face of George Washington (don't tell your father, but Caroline and I think it looks more like a horse's head). Please pick up pen and paper and write again soon.

WITH AFFECTION,

MISS BET

OCTOBER 15, 1859

I've decided to marry Wilson. Can't let on, though . . . I might scare him away. Don't want Miss Bet to find out, either. She wouldn't understand, since she's never been in love. And Mama and Daddy would pitch a fit if they knew. They'd say I was only thirteen and acting foolish.

Well, what if I am? All I know is that Wilson is the most upstanding boy I've ever met. Too upstanding . . . I can't even get him to hold my hand.

He's called on me at least once a week since the Frederick Douglass lecture. On Sundays we usually walk to one of the creeks over in Fairmount Park. We hardly see anybody down there, so I don't have to be so goody-goody. Like today, when I kicked off my shoes to stomp and splash in the water.

Wilson shook his head from the bank. He couldn't believe I was having such fun, but that's because boys wear pants and can do whatever they want.

"What if the Widow could see you now, Liza?" he called. "She would be mortified that you are showing your legs."

Wilson's too serious! Sometimes I like to shake a little devilment into him, so I lifted my skirts a few inches.

When he helped me up the bank, he wiped creek water from my face with his handkerchief. My stomach felt quivery—sort of hot and chilly, all at once. Lordy, I sure wish Wilson would kiss me sometime.

2311 E. GRACE STREET

RICHMOND, VIRGINIA

OCTOBER 20, 1859

Dear Liza,

Not a line from you in over six weeks! Are you studying too hard, dear?

I write to ask if there is news in Philadelphia of John Brown and his army of Negroes, as this business has upset everyone in the house. The newspapers here say he is a fanatic. They consider his attack three days ago on the Federal arsenal at Harpers Ferry, Virginia, an invasion of the South. Only a madman, they claim, would try to free millions of slaves with a few runaways and a handful of guns.

I do not think what he did was right, Liza, but he has suffered as one with the slaves. Pray that the Virginia governor will spare his life. And when you can, send us something truthful to read about this courageous Brown.

MISS BET

27 CHESTNUT STREET

PHILADELPHIA, PENNSYLVANIA

DECEMBER 4, 1859

Dear Miss Bet,

Better find a bucket for your tears. I know you'll cry like I did when you read this broadside. A close friend of mine (he's very smart) says we should pray for John Brown. That he doesn't know of any other white person who would die so slaves could go free.

But maybe we should pray for John Brown's body. Did you know that after the court hanged Brown in Charles Town, Virginia, they refused to embalm the corpse? So a Philadelphia abolitionist said an undertaker would tend to it here.

Out of respect, my friend and I met the train carrying Brown's remains. When we arrived at the Broad Street depot, antislavery people were already standing three and four deep on the sidewalk. An icy wind from the river scalded our cheeks, but we didn't mind.

Then the train chugged into the station, and a gang of young white men started shoving to get in front. They even knocked a few people down. Somebody in the crowd said they were Southern students from the Medical College of Pennsylvania.

Cowards. I could have choked the mess out of them. They'd never have the grit to do what John Brown did.

"Let us take his body," they hollered, loud enough for the dead man himself to hear them. "We know what to do with it!"

Think of it, Miss Bet! John Brown's wife was sitting on the train and hearing all this.

"Get back," the police warned. There was a terrible scuffle and, they had to use billy clubs. My friend hurried us back to the carriage, and as we ran, I spotted this broadside lying in a gutter. The rest of it is probably under some proslavery boot.

Today my history teacher said she heard a rumor that the police tricked the crowd. While two policemen unloaded a decoy coffin from the train, others sneaked the real coffin down to the wharf and onto a boat. So John Brown went on to New York, his sad, dead flesh rotting away. Miss Bet, I've been telling you the folks in this city are cruel. Maybe you'll believe me now.

And I'll tell you what else is the truth. John Brown woke up a lot of sleeping abolitionists in Philadelphia. Before his raid, most white antislavery people had turned colder than yesterday's coffee. They wouldn't even risk coming to a meeting, now that the city is run over with Southern sympathizers. Brown's death put the fire back in their voices, though.

Maybe it's not in the Richmond papers yet—did you know he handed the guard a note just before they hanged him?

"I, John Brown," it said, "am now quite certain that the crimes

of this guilty land *will never be purged* away *but with blood."*
Guilt and blood . . . Brown has left us something sizable to think
about, Miss Bet. As Daddy would say, "He may be dead, but he
ain't gone."

YOURS TRULY,

LIZA

ADDRESS OF JOHN BROWN

To the Virginia Court, when about to receive the

SENTENCE OF DEATH,

For his heroic attempt at Harper's Ferry, to

Give deliverance to the captives, and to let the oppressed go free.

I have, may it please the Court, a few words to say.

In the first place, I deny every thing but what I have already admitted, of a design on my part to *free Slaves.* I intended, certainly, to have made a clean thing of that matter, as I did last winter, when I went into Missouri, and there took Slaves, without the snapping of a gun on either side, moving them through the country, and finally leaving them in Canada. I desired to have done the same thing again on a much larger scale. *That was all I intended.* I never did intend murder, or treason, or the destruction of property, or to excite or incite Slaves to rebellion, or to make insurrection.

I say I am yet too young to understand that GOD is any *respecter of persons.* I believe that to have interfered as I have done, as I have always freely admitted I have done, in behalf of his *despised poor,* I have done no wrong, but right.

Now, if it is deemed necessary that I should forfeit my life, for the furtherance of the ends of justice, and MINGLE MY BLOOD FURTHER WITH THE BLOOD OF MY CHILDREN, and with the blood of millions in this Slave country, whose rights are disregarded by wicked, cruel, and unjust enactments,—I say, LET IT BE DONE.

Let me say one word furt... satisfied

27 CHESTNUT STREET

PHILADELPHIA, PENNSYLVANIA

JULY 15, 1860

Dear Miss Bet,

Thank you for letting me spend the summer in Philadelphia. I just wish you'd bring Mama and Daddy up here to visit like I asked. There's somebody I want y'all to meet, and something we want to tell you. He's so bright, Miss Bet. I know you'd like talking to him about politics.

Wilson (that's his name—Wilson Bowser) is all excited about Abraham Lincoln running for president. He says the Southern states are full of bluster. That if Lincoln wins, they won't really leave the Union like they say they will. What do you think, Miss Bet?

LIZA

27 CHESTNUT STREET

PHILADELPHIA, PENNSYLVANIA

AUGUST 12, 1860

Dear Miss Bet,

Since it looks like you're too busy to visit me, I have to do this by letter. Wilson Bowser and I are engaged, and we want your permission to marry next spring. He'll be finished with school by then. I'll only have one year to go.

Now don't go flying off the handle, Miss Bet. Once you meet Wilson, I know you'll approve.

LOVE,

LIZA

WHITE SULPHUR SPRINGS, VIRGINIA

AUGUST 30, 1860

Dear Liza,

Rec'd your request today. No, you do not have permission to marry this Wilson whatever-his-name-is next spring. I do not care if he is a Richmond boy. A girl of fourteen is too young to know her own mind on romantic matters. I have discussed it with your parents, and they agree.

In love? I think you are in love with a wedding cake and a white taffeta dress. You say he is mannerable, with a strong chin and honest eyes? Believe me, a handsome face can hide many faults.

Besides, I have enough to worry about as it is. Signs of war are everywhere in Virginia, even here at the White. This morning I heard Edmund Ruffin, a farmer from the Shenandoah Valley, shouting under the oaks. With his long white hair and staring eyes of a statue, Ruffin looked quite the lunatic. Yet a willing audience of hundreds applauded every phrase and stood in line to buy his photograph.

"Fellow citizens!" he ranted. "God has ordained that you own slaves! Will you submit to Yankees stealing your property?"

I hovered at the back and itched to speak out, until a member of the Virginia House of Delegates shouted, "Anyone who thinks slavery is wrong should be hung!" I am ashamed to say that fear froze my tongue.

And now Mother has shut the window that looks out over the hotel common. She is complaining that blasts of musket fire are giving her an earache. It is Company F of the Richmond Volunteers . . . one hundred foolhardy young men who have come to the White to drill for war.

Liza, let this photograph of Ruffin serve as a reminder—hate has boiled the brains of our people. Finish your schooling. Then we will discuss marriage.

WITH WORRIED AFFECTION,

MISS BET

P.S. I am returning the sketch of your wedding dress. Caroline will not be making it for a long while.

MARCH 1, 1861

Telegram from Liza received today. She is too young, too young! Doesn't she realize that seven Southern states have seceded from the Union? This is certainly no time to start a marriage.

"Tell Mama to make dress. Wilson and I coming home April 14. Will return to live in Philadelphia after wedding."

APRIL 12, 1861

1 P.M.

I do not feel at all well. James just dashed in with a newspaper extra. S. C. militia cannoned Federal troops at Fort Sumter at 4:30 this morning. That fool, Edmund Ruffin, fired the opening shot. God save us.

APRIL 13, 1861

4:30 P.M.

Federal troops surrendered the fort at noon today, and hysteria reigns here in the city. Buglers playing "Dixie" are marching toward Main, preceded by a Confederate flag. Hundreds of residents have left their houses to follow. They seem inhuman as they rattle by . . . dry, faceless sticks, ready to burst into flame.

Do I imagine that some slow down to stare at the Van Lew mansion? Only a two-feet-high iron fence separates us from the street, and the ornamental spears wouldn't stop a cat. Anyone with a grudge against abolitionists could jump it and bound up our curved steps in a moment. I do not share these thoughts with Mother.

Nelson has headed out to see where the mob plans to go. I begged him to stay in safety with us.

"Miss Bet," he said, "I've been outsmarting Richmond white folks all my life. Ain't nothing these seceshes can do to me that they haven't tried before."

So here we women sit, butterflies pinned in a case. Mary has shuttered the windows and drawn the velvet curtains. Mother is paler than January, and I cannot find a chair big enough to hold my fear.

"Bet, stop that pacing," Mother said. "You will rub a hole in the Persian rug. Nelson can take care of himself . . . and please stop biting your nails."

But much more than Nelson is on my mind. When Caroline served tea, we exchanged an anxious look over the silver tray. If only Liza had listened to me and postponed this ridiculous wedding! May God protect my child from war-crazed passengers, for I doubt her young man can do it.

---

6 P.M.

Nelson just returned to the sound of gunfire.

"Shots!" Mother cried. "Is this war already?"

"It's a hundred-cannon salute, Mrs. Van Lew, down on the canal by Tredegar Iron Works." Nelson's face was glazed with sweat. He must have run the twenty blocks back, though he is too much a man to admit it.

"There was plenty of speechifying about Tredegar," he said, "and how it's the South's largest foundry. That Tredegar cannons sent the Yankees at Fort Sumter packing to New York." Caroline dabbed his face with a tea towel and led him to a chair.

"Someone in the crowd raised the Confederate Stars and Bars, Miss Bet. Now they're planning to fly it over the Capitol. Folks is pretty riled up. Some are armed, and more'n a few are drunk as Cootie Brown. Nobody's in the mood for free black faces. Thought I'd best come on home."

So the traitors have removed the United States flag. Still, there may be hope for my beloved Virginia. The secession convention hasn't voted yet to leave the Union. Fully two-thirds of the delegates are unwilling to be dumb sheep and follow the Cotton States over a cliff of destruction.

Yesterday I sat in on the speeches and saw delegates from western Virginia wipe away tears. Surely they will vote with their hearts. Surely Liza will step off that train tomorrow, smiling and safe.

APRIL 16, 1861

9 A.M.

My wedding day!

I didn't think I'd need to write in my book anymore, now that I've got Wilson to talk to. But Miss Bet's grip on me is tighter than a corset. I've got to figure out how to make her let go.

As soon as we got off the train on Saturday, I knew the wedding would be complicated. First she smothered me with questions about medical students riding the train with us from Philadelphia.

"The paper said two hundred and fifty Virginia boys were coming home to fight. . . . Were they rude. . . ? Did they hurt you?"

Wilson tried to tell Miss Bet they were too busy singing "Dixie" to bother with us, but she didn't seem to know he was there. Then she started in on the wedding. "Everything's taken care of," she declared. Mama told me later that planning the party has kept Miss Bet busy as a hen with one chick.

She's got Mary polishing silver and washing cut-glass bowls, and for days, Mama's been working on the food: orange baskets with candied violets, chicken croquettes, water ices, even Roman punch. And Miss Bet's trying to have the wedding at St. John's.

"You'd be the first colored couple to get married there," Mama told Wilson and me last night. "I think this is Miss Bet's way of getting even with people who've snubbed the Van Lews. Last Sunday Mrs. Potts sat in front of us at church."

"'It's one thing to let coloreds attend service,'" she whispered to her husband. 'It's quite another to be married here!'"

"Mama, you think they'll let us go through with it?"

"Sure, honey," she said. "Miss Bet's name and money will win out, don't you worry."

Miss Bet hasn't really talked to Wilson since we arrived, except to ask him a string of questions about his folks and his education and will we try to get back to Philadelphia so I can finish school but maybe that would be too risky now and wouldn't he like to work at one of the hardware stores?

And she keeps pressing me to teach free black children in the neighborhood. That way Wilson and I could live in the mansion until this war talk is settled, and this would suit everyone, wouldn't it? I didn't bother telling her again that I don't want to be a teacher. She wouldn't listen.

So I've tried to forget about Miss Bet and her questions. Almost did, until early this morning. Mama was curling my hair by the stove.

"Could you fix it just like those ladies in the *Godey's Book*?" I asked.

Mama ignored me and kept on twisting and sizzling. "Last time I fixed your hair was the morning you left for Philadelphia," she said. "Remember? You'd just turned ten. All you needed then were two plaits and some bows. Now you got me sweating over these wishbone irons trying to make you look grown up."

"I *am* grown up," I reminded her.

She shook her head and gave me a hand mirror. I was so busy smiling at the ringlets that I didn't hear Miss Bet come in. I saw her through the mirror, standing in the doorway with a flabby smile on her face. So! I thought. She's finally decided to say something nice.

"Morning, Miss Bet," Mama said. "Don't my little girl look pretty?" Doggone! Between Mama and Miss Bet, I guess I'll be ten years old forever.

Miss Bet laid an armful of pink camellias in my lap. "These are for your bouquet, Liza."

I have to admit they were lovely. Wrapped with white ribbons and smelling so sweet. I buried my face in them and took a deep breath. "Thank you, Miss Bet. They're perfect."

"Have you and that young man—"

"Wilson," I corrected.

"Wilson, found a place to live?"

"Yesterday Wilson went looking for work at the Exchange Hotel," I said. "He met a woman heading out the back door as he went in. They got to talking, and she's going to let us have a room in her house on Locust Alley, down toward the river in Shockoe Bottom. Her name's Clara Coleman."

"Liza, I forbid this! Land's sake, Shockoe Bottom is a nest of beer saloons and gambling halls. The neighborhood is most unsafe."

Mama jumped at the word "unsafe," and Miss Bet looked to her for help. Mama kept quiet. I guess she knows by now I can argue for myself.

"Yes, but Wilson wants us to be on our own—he even turned down his parents when they asked us to stay with them. And suppose the rooming houses weren't filled with convention people. They still wouldn't want coloreds. Only other places for Negroes to rent are shanties in Butcher Town or Screamersville. Besides," I said, "Miss Coleman won't charge us if I help around the house and go to the market every day. She'll let us use her kitchen, too."

I could tell Miss Bet was getting agitated. She started biting her nails, right down to the quick.

"I insist that you and Wilson stay here at the mansion, under my care. The streets are full of drunken soldiers. They are fired up with secession talk and looking for a fight."

"You can't scare me, Miss Bet. I'm getting married at four o'clock today, and I'll be in the care of my husband. It's too late to make me do anything!"

I still can't believe I did it—I threw the bouquet right at Miss Bet's feet. It felt so good to do that! A good many stems snapped against her skirts, and some flower heads rolled across the floor.

I'm not sure, but I think Miss Bet's eyes watered, and after she stalked out, I cried, too. Poor broken-neck flowers. And my wedding day, already ruined.

Mama sat me down at the table. "Liza, God has given you a rainbow, and you're chasing after waterfalls. He's found you a fine young man to marry, and that's all that matters. I just wish he hadn't found you one so soon."

"But, Miss Bet, she's got no call to—"

"Baby, I know her better than she knows herself. Ignore her when she starts acting two-headed. I do, and it's saved us many a sharp word."

I guess Mama's right—I shouldn't worry about Miss Bet. I should be looking forward to my wedding night. I told Wilson I was a little anxious about it, and he said we won't do anything until we're both ready, and I said, "Well, Wilson, how will we know when we're ready?" He said, "Liza, quit asking so many questions." Wilson never cuts me off like that. He must be anxious, too.

6 P.M.

Got to hurry. Wilson's waiting to take me to Miss Clara's house, but I want to paste our marriage license here in the album. He thinks it's silly, but I won't feel married until my scrapbook knows about it.

The ceremony was sweeter than honeysuckle, in spite of Miss Bet's meddling. She had a fat look around her eyes, like she'd been crying a lot, but neither of us let on that we'd had cross words. Mama talked me into carrying what was left of the bouquet, and the churchyard looked like a fairyland, with dogwood and cherry blossoms everywhere.

Just a few folks came—our mamas and daddies, Mary and James, Bob and Oliver from the farm. Miss Bet's mother, and Brother John, too. I haven't seen him since I was a little girl. Wilson liked him right away. Says he's a generous soul, and he must be, because he gave us a gift of money and wished us a happy life together. They've all gone now, and so must I. Good-bye, scrapbook, good-bye, good-bye! Won't need you anymore!

MARRIAGE LICENSE.

Whereas, application has been made to me by *Wilson Bowser* of *Richmond City*, and *Mary Elizabeth Van Lew* of *Richmond City*, for License to be joined in Holy Matrimony, **These are therefore to Authorise and License** you to solemnize the Rites of Marriage between the said persons, according to Law, there appearing to you no lawful cause or just impediment, by reason of consanguinity or affinity to hinder the same.

Given under my Hand and the Seal of my Office, this *16th* day of *April* in the year eighteen hundred and sixty *one.*

.... *W. J. Hamill* ....
Clerk of the Hustings Court

.... *S. L. Farrat* ....

To the Rev. Mr. *Echolls* ....
OR ANY PERSON QUALIFIED BY LAW TO CELEBRATE THE
MARRIAGE RITE IN THE STATE OF VIRGINIA.

License	$4.00
Clerk's Fee	.50
Total	$4.50

55

APRIL 17, 1861

The Virginia governor has announced secession. President Lincoln has called for seventy-five thousand troops to defend the Union. Oh, my lost country! My lost child!

APRIL 20, 1861

Flyer found by Mary on our doorstep this morning. Well, they wanted war—now they have it.

DEFENCE OF OUR CAPITAL
NO SURRENDER
UNDER ANY CIRCUMSTANCES!

All Officers and Soldiers not now in service, and all citizens of the State and Confederate States not enrolled in the 2nd Class Militia, are requested to enroll their names to-day at the City Hall, as members of the new organization now being raised under the proclamation of the Governor for the defence of this city.

Dear album, I guess I was wrong. Why did I think I could live without you? It's lonely here at Miss Clara's. Wilson goes out every day to look for a job that pays decent . . . comes home saying there's nothing for free Negroes except manual labor. He can't wait to go back to Philadelphia, where he can use his education. I worry that he blames me for being stuck here in Richmond, now that the war has started.

"The war won't last long," Wilson assured me last night. "When it's safe for free Negroes to travel again, we'll return. Anyway, it's you I need in my life now."

Then he teased me and said we should practice kissing. He thinks we need to work on it all we can since we're new at it. He says I should work on my cooking, too, because Mama spoiled me by not making me help in the kitchen, and that's why I burn his breakfast eggs. Ask me, he's too picky about those eggs.

Miss Clara is real good-natured. First day she told us to call her Miss Clara. Said Coleman sounds too formal. And she gave us a room on the third floor so we can all have privacy, she said. The room is no bigger than a sparrow's nest. Wilson and I have squeezed in a bed, two chairs, and a slab table. It's plenty cramped, but at least we're together.

I like going to the market for Miss Clara. It's not easy, though. Everything costs too much, and I have to haggle with the vendors until I get the freshest bread and tenderest greens. Everybody's talking about the fine crops this year—corn, vegetables, fruits—and how the best is going to warehouses for the Rebel soldiers. I wish they'd leave a little something for other folk.

On my way out this morning, two washerwomen passed by Miss Clara's front door. They sounded like crows when a hawk flies by. One pointed at the house. "There lives a lady of the night," she said.

"Clara Coleman should be locked up," cawed the other.

I didn't think it was any of their business how late Miss Clara stays up, so I asked Wilson about it after supper. Now that he's told me men pay ladies of the night to keep them company, I'm glad Miss Clara put us on the top floor.

The drunken soldiers Miss Bet warned me about are pretty rowdy. The streets in Shockoe are crawling with them, like maggots in a ham hock. I stay close to Miss Clara's except on Sundays, when Wilson and I visit Mama and Daddy at the kitchen house.

It seems strange not to walk up the path to the mansion and visit Miss Bet, too, but I'm not ready for another fight. I miss her every now and then. If only she weren't so . . . so . . . in charge! If, if, if. Well, Mama says if a bullfrog had wings, he wouldn't flop his behind against the ground.

Husband—"Mary, my love, this apple-dumpling is not half-done." Wife—"Well, finish it, then, my dear."

JUNE 16, 1861

After church, Nelson drove Mother and me over to the old fairground, which is now called Camp Lee. I wanted to ride by Clara Coleman's house and inspect it, but Mother has been anxious about the strength of Lee's army. It is hard to tell, as the entire city is awash in soldiers.

We left Nelson with the carriage and walked into a scene of utter confusion. The fairground seemed to be in constant motion—a monstrous animal with many limbs writhing at once. Yet I must remember that the monster has a heart.

Each company of one hundred men occupies a camp "street," with tents on either side and a larger captain's tent at the end. The wealthier men have horses, guns, and manservants to care for their uniforms. Other companies are composed of humble fellows who have been tricked into fighting a slaveholders' war.

Mother turned down one of these less prosperous streets, and I followed. Undershirts and drawers were thrown over the tents to dry. A few soldiers were breaking the Sabbath and playing cards.

She paused to visit with a farm boy crouched at a campfire.

"Afternoon, ma'am," he said, nodding. As he smiled, a field of freckles bloomed across his face.

"And the same to you," Mother replied. "May I ask your name?"

"Jim," he said. When he stood up, his large hands flopped like fish into his overall pockets. "Private Jim Coffey."

"Well, Jim Coffey, you must have a mother who misses you today."

"Yes'm, I do," he said. "My folks and me raise 'baccy on a farm over near Lynchburg."

"Then why are you here? Shouldn't you be helping with spring planting?"

"I'm here to protect ladies like you, a'course!" he answered. "Mr. Lincoln's gonna come down here and set all the Nigras free. The newspapers say so! Who knows what the coloreds will do then?"

His words were so absurd that I smiled. I wanted to tell him about our wise, gentle Nelson, but Mother interrupted. "And have you arms?" she asked.

"Nothing except a bowie knife." His voice had a proud mountain ring. "The state's gonna give me what I need to kill a Yankee."

So innocent! Not much older than Liza, for all that she's trying to act twice her age.

"God bless you, son," Mother said, and we left him then, both of us low in spirit.

"Bet," she said, sighing, as we moved through the dusty camp streets, "I cannot picture that boy with a bayonet in his chest."

"There is nothing to be done for the Rebels, Mother. I think we must resolve to help the Union now. Together you and Brother John and I have almost two hundred thousand dollars. Perhaps we could start by giving money to the war effort in Washington."

"Good gracious, Bet! How would we send it? A bank draft made out to President Lincoln? What if the Confederates check our mail?"

"We have to take the risk. How can we sit by and watch the Rebels destroy our country?"

For now, I will hide my true thoughts from Mother. By the name of my long-gone friend, Fannie, I shall fight this rebellion any way I can. No task will be too small or too dangerous. Surely there are others who will help. At the very least, I know I can trust the Lohmann family, City Councillor Haskins, Mrs. Carrington, Dr. McCaw. Every opportunity shall be *my* bowie knife, *my* musket. Money is only the first step.

The words seem cruel as I write them. What if a Van Lew dollar buys the bullet that maims Jim Coffey? Or kills A. T.? I feel certain he has signed up to fight for the precious Cause. Despite myself, I looked for his curly head in the throngs of horses and men. No sign, and it's just as well. Better to see him dead than wearing a Confederate uniform.

JULY 12, 1861

This miserable war. The Confederates are making Wilson work at Tredegar Iron Works. They say he's eligible since he's not attached as a servant to a white household. Wish I hadn't been so pigheaded. Should have done like Miss Bet asked. If Wilson is making cannons to use against the Union, it's all my fault.

My husband and I don't talk much these days. He's too tired from sweating in the foundry, twelve hours a day, seven days a week. Confederates claim they're so holy, but don't think anything about using folks on Sundays. Can't give God one day.

I planted a morning glory vine by Miss Clara's back stoop. It's nothing at all like the boxwoods in Miss Bet's grand garden, but at least it's mine.

JULY 25, 1861

A bright, pleasant day. Temperature exactly right. How can this be, when everything else has gone wrong? Union defeat at Manassas and despair in my heart.

Exactly three months and one week since I have seen Liza. Have I lost her forever? Where is the tiny girl who clung to my skirts and begged for a story? The cherub who used to surprise me in the garden with gifts of rocks and berries?

UNION OF THE SOUTH

NEWS BY TELEGRAPH.

REPORTED FOR THE RICHMOND ENQUIRER.

BATTLE NEAR MANASSA!

THE SOUTHERN TROOPS VICTORIOUS

THE ENEMY ROUTED AND IN FULL RETREAT.

Southern Cavalry in Close Pursuit.

MANASSA, July 21.—A ten hour battle was fought to-day at the Stone Bridge. General Beauregard was victorious.

The slaughter on both sides was tremendous. Beauregard had his horse killed under him while leading Gen. Wade Hampton's Legion into action. Gen. Johnston seized the colors of a wavering Regiment, and rallied them to the charge. It is impossible to estimate the number of killed and wounded.

Sherman's celebrated Battery of Light Artillery was taken by our troops.

It is reported that the Federal Commander, General McDowell, is mortally wounded. On our side Colonel and acting Brigadier General Francis S. Bartow, of Georgia, was seriously wounded.

The battle commenced at eight A. M. and closed at six P. M.—the enemy in full retreat and pursued by our cavalry. President Davis arrived on the battle field after the action.

SECOND DESPATCH.

MANASSA, July 21——The battle commenced at 8 o'clock Sunday morning, and became general about noon, and the engagement closed at 6 o'clock, P. M. The left wing was commanded by Gen. Johnston, the right by Gen. Beauregard.

The fight was very severe and fatal on both sides. Among the prominent officers who are reported to have been killed, are Gen. Bee, of South Carolina, Brigadier General Kirby Smith, of Florida, and Lieut. Col. Johnson, of the Hampton Legion.

Beauregard and staff are safe.

THIRD DSEPATCH.

Sherman's battery is said to have been taken by the 4th Alabama Regiment, which was cut up fearfully. Other accounts say that the battery was taken by the Virginia 17th Regiment. Whichever it was, it is said they charged gallantly up to the mouths of the guns, and took them.

On our side Generals Bee, of South Carolina, and Smith, of Florida, have fallen. It is said Col. Bartow is seriously wounded. Lt. Col. Johnson, of Hampton's Legion, was killed.

Northern Account of the Battle near Manassa.

Dear Miss Bet,

If I didn't think we'd fight, I'd come see you myself, but we both know how that tune would play, so I'm sending you a note. Since the Battle of Manassas, I've heard rumors about you and Mrs. Van Lew. When I read The Enquirer *this morning, I found out they were true.*

Now you've gone and got yourself in the paper as a Union sympathizer! I know you probably read the same article I did, but I'm sending you a copy since you don't always hear what folks tell you. Miss Bet, pay attention. The Rebels are hanging people who're not on their side.

LIZA

THE DAILY RICHMOND ENQUIRER
JULY 31, 1861

Two ladies, mother and daughter, living on Church Hill, have lately attracted public notice by their attentions to the Yankee prisoners confined in this city. Whilst every true woman in this community has been busy making articles of comfort or necessity for our troops, these two women have been expending their money in aiding and giving comfort to the criminals who have invaded our sacred soil, bent on raping and murder, the desolation of our homes and sacred places, and the ruin and dishonour of our families.

The Yankee wounded have been put under charge of competent surgeons and provided with good nurses. This is more than they deserve and have any right to expect, and the course of these two females in providing them with delicacies, buying them books, stationery and paper, cannot but be regarded as an evidence of sympathy amounting to the endorsement of the cause and conduct of these Northern Vandals.

Dear Liza,

How I rejoiced when your note arrived. Even as I opened the envelope, I was thinking of a reply . . . some brief words of regret for disrupting your wedding day. When I saw no apology for throwing the flowers at me, I shook the envelope. Surely a page is missing, I thought, but I was wrong. Liza, you know better. How many times have I heard Nelson say, "When you mess up, Liza, you 'fess up'"?

Please do not bother with more warnings. Without an apology, they would mean little. Yes, it is dangerous to flaunt my Union sympathies. I am in agony over poor William Roane . . . I fear they hanged my former slave out of revenge, since they cannot prove any treason committed by me.

But the Union officers inside Harwood Prison are scared and homesick. They need stationery and books to pass the dreary hours. It is the least I can do.

My visits to Harwood will continue as long as the guards allow. Despite my reputation as an abolitionist, it is quite easy to sweet-talk them with food. A pan of Caroline's gingerbread, a glass of buttermilk, and the doors open wide.

MISS BET

SEPTEMBER 7, 1861

8 P.M.

If not for Nelson, I would break my vow.

This afternoon he found me behind the oak tree in the garden, ripping open the spine of Bunyan's *Holy War.*

"Miss Bet! What you doing? Your daddy's bones would rise up if he saw you hurting one of his books."

I glanced up at the house. No one was on the veranda. "Sit down, Nelson." I made a place for him on the bench. "This morning I left books with the prisoners and picked up ones they have read. One of the men gripped my hand tightly as he placed the book in my basket. I suspect there is a message hidden inside, for the top of this spine has come loose from the binding."

"Let me help you." Nelson pulled out his pocketknife and wedged open the spine. "Well, look here," he said, pulling out a folded square of paper. "This your stationery, Miss Bet? Why, them words ain't no bigger than cake crumbs."

I read the message aloud. "'N.Y. Congressman Alfred Huson taken prisoner at Manassas. He is deathly ill. Can you get him out?'"

"Huson is a civilian!" I cried. "They have no right to keep him." Then panic swept over me. Who else of my heart and home might the Confederates hang if I bring a Yankee to the house? Nelson patted my hand when it started to shake. "Just be bold, Miss Bet. Go right on down to the boss man of the prison. Ask him straight out if you can nurse this Yankee here at the mansion. Boss ain't going to cross a fine lady like you."

"Yes, but then the entire family will be involved. They are suffering enough as it is. John says business is off at the hardware stores, and

Mother is quite lonely—when she calls on old friends, few will receive her. And you and Caroline . . . think of what they did to William Roane!"

Nelson stood up to make his final pronouncement. "Thought I knew you better, Miss Bet. Remember when your daddy took ill back in 'forty? He was too sick to notice that my runaway friend, Beverly, was hiding in your basement. Wasn't it you who nursed Beverly's bad knee, gave him new clothes before he ran off to the North? I'll handle Caroline, Miss Bet. You do what you need to do . . . 'less you got a wishbone for a backbone."

Shame warmed my face as he walked back to the kitchen house, and his words are with me still. Flowers and books for the prisoners are not enough. I must hide behind these simple kindnesses to do the real work of war. I hear Mother coming to bed. If she is willing to take in Mr. Huson, then so shall I.

LOCUST ALLEY

OCTOBER 14, 1861

Miss Bet, have you lost your buttons? Some rough-looking Johnny Rebs came to visit Miss Clara. While they were waiting in the parlor, I overheard them talking about you. They said you've been nursing a Northern civilian captured at Bull Run. That he's been piled up in one of your four-poster beds for weeks, and you and Mrs. Van Lew were wiping his "filthy Yankee brow" all that time.

"Don't care how rich the Van Lews are," they growled. "Somebody should jerk them women up and teach 'em how to be real Southerners."

And they said the sick man died today, and y'all have buried him in the Van Lew family plot! Maybe you don't care about yourself or Mrs. Van Lew's safety, but people think your servants are Van Lews, too. Can't you consider my folks for a change?

LIZA

Miss Bet, you're about to worry the stuffing out of me. Mama visited today, looking upset. "Liza," she said, "a lot of Feds were captured yesterday in that battle near Leesburg."

I said, "I know, and what's that got to do with you, Mama," and she said, "Miss Bet and another lady went out to the road to see the Yankee prisoners marched into town. Gave them a real good welcoming, with food and flowers and books to read while they locked up.

"I told Nelson it don't look right," Mama went on, "and he said don't be alarmed, since Miss Bet was on a mission of mercy, and, anyway, the lady with her was the wife of a Confederate general."

Mama fidgeted in the chair like she was sitting on a hot biscuit. "Miss Bet's got her fingers in too many Northern pies, and folks won't stand for it. I can feel it in my bones. They goin' to burn us all in our beds one night!"

If there's one thing I trust, it's the feeling Mama gets in her bones. I don't want to lose you, Miss Bet, even if you are as stubborn as a sticky drawer. And I sure don't want to see Mama and Daddy blindfolded and led to the gallows with you.

Maybe there haven't been any "I'm sorrys" between us, but we've got bigger cabbages to tend now. Act like a rich Southern woman is supposed to act. Stay in the house and mind your own business!

LIZA

Dear Liza,

I declare, your warnings have been most annoying. However, your concern makes me think I can beg for your help. Today I visited Harwood again. The guards looked through their sign-in book and said they saw my name too many times. They say I should not come back, but, Liza, many of the officers inside are raging with fever. I have been thinking that Caroline's rich egg custard would be of some comfort. God knows, they need nourishment, since rancid bacon and wormy soup are the usual rations.

If you would accompany me when I take the custard, I would refer to you as a slave I have recently bought. Perhaps they would think I have rejoined the fold and am simply a good Southern woman on an errand of mercy. It might not work, but I am desperate to try anything. There is one more problem. Your mother refuses to make the dish.

"Miss Bet," she said in the dining room this morning, "you'll hang with a custard bowl in your hand, and I won't have that on my conscience."

Would you speak to her, Liza? I must *bring something to the prisoners. I trust you realize this war is bigger than either of us. Please, this once . . . do as I ask.*

Miss Bet

Dear Miss Bet,

You're crazier than that cuckoo bird in your papa's clock. I'm free now, and I won't go back to being a slave, not even for an hour.

Leave Mama out of your scheme. What if somebody found out she was making custard for Union men? Don't cross me on this, Miss Bet, or I'll convince Daddy and her to work elsewhere.

Mama could stem tobacco as easily as strip your collards, and Daddy might prefer cutting hair in a barber shop to pruning your shrubs.

Here's the custard recipe. You make it yourself.

LIZA

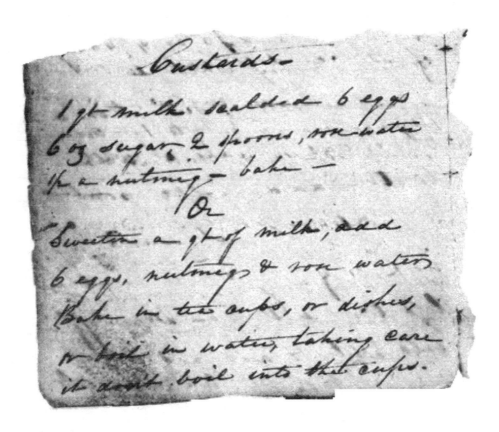

DECEMBER 25, 1861

Freezing day, with not a bird or squirrel in sight. All my Christmas happy is gone, too. The morning started out sweet enough. Wilson gave me a set of color pencils for drawing in this book, and I made him a silk neckerchief. We walked up Church Hill and took presents to Mama and Daddy.

So Mama says as she's serving pound cake, "Liza, ain't it time you made up with Miss Bet? She's home from church and in the mansion right now, opening presents with her mother and John and all."

And Daddy says, "Your mama's right. What better day to remember that Christ is part of the word 'Christmas'?" Daddy poured some coffee in his saucer. "Yesterday Miss Bet reminded me there's a favor she's been wanting you to do. Something about going somewhere with her."

"Another slice of cake, Wilson?" I said, hoping to change the subject. I wasn't about to tell Daddy that Miss Bet wants me to be her pretend slave. He'd never want me to do such a thing.

"Whatever it is, might make a good Christmas present," Daddy added.

He sure seems fixed on me doing this favor for Miss Bet. Why can't she ever ever ever take no for an answer? And why is she so stuck on this custard business, anyway?

LOCUST ALLEY

JANUARY 20, 1862

Wish I'd taken a different route to the market this morning. Wish I hadn't seen the red flag flapping outside the Odd Fellows Hall. I'll never forget that man's voice coming through the open window.

"How much, gentlemen?" he barked. "Bid up, bid up!"

How was I to know it was a slave auction? Mama kept me away from them when I was little, so I only heard about them at lectures in Philadelphia. If I remember everything exactly, I can tell Wilson when he gets home, and if I tell him, maybe I can get past the awfulness of it.

The colored men sat on one side, the women on the other. The younger men were stripped to the waist and smeared with lard. Don't know why. It must make them look healthier.

Some were laughing and dancing like they were happy to be slaves. Made no sense until I saw a slave trader in the next pen pouring whiskey down a black man's throat. I wonder why people take liquor. From the man's tears, looked to me like it must hurt to drink it.

Then I saw a woman climb on top of a rickety crate. The auctioneer invited those greasy white men to step up and examine a "prime breeder." They lifted her skirts to check for leg boils. They probed her mouth, like they were putting in a horse bit.

She hardly seemed to know where she was. Kept working her lips and looking over at the next pen. Never took her eyes off it, and I finally figured out why. It was her man who was choking on that whiskey. It was him they were going to sell next, after they'd taken one thousand dollars for her flesh.

How will I tell Wilson this next part, when I can barely write the words? Her name was Liza! Same as mine. It could have been me up on that crate. Could have been Wilson gagging on forced liquor. I felt like Lot's wife in the Bible. The one who turns into a pillar of salt when she looks at something she isn't supposed to see.

I was a slobbery mess when I got home, crying and heaving with a sick stomach. Miss Clara fiddled and fussed and begged me to tell her what was wrong. After I told her where I'd been, she didn't ask anything else. I guess Miss Clara's seen it all before.

She led me to the settee in her bedroom and handed me a cup of ginger tea. Then she pulled the curtains and closed the door. "Honey, I've been waiting for the right time to tell you this." Her buttery soft voice calmed me down some. I like Miss Clara, because I know she likes me. Her hair is too bright, but Wilson says there's a good person under all that dye and face rouge.

"I've heard a lot about your Miss Bet and, like her, I'm against the brutal crime you saw today. But nobody knows how I feel, especially the doo-dah Confederate officials who visit late at night. All they know is, I'm the best woman in Richmond to keep them company."

Miss Clara chuckled. "Just this morning at dawn, General Winder slipped out the back door. He's in charge of Confederate prisons. Even Judah Benjamin, the Confederate Secretary of War, visits me. That man must love to eat—I call him 'Big Belly.'"

Laughing made Miss Clara seem younger. She usually looks so tired.

"I want you to tell Miss Bet about these fine officials, these Southern gentlemen who pay for my services with new blankets and medicinal wine meant for Rebel soldiers. The information could be useful to her someday, and she might not listen to a . . . a businesswoman like me."

I sat up real straight. "Miss Bet and I don't see or speak to each other, Miss Clara. She's too hard to get along with. Bossy and all."

Her kind brown eyes wouldn't let mine go. She reminded me of Mama, when Mama means for me to listen and not talk back. "Help her, sugar," Miss Clara said softly. "Help her all you can."

Now I don't know what to do. If I go with Miss Bet to the prison like she asked, I'll have to be a make-believe slave. And if I tell her the secrets on

Benjamin and Winder, I'll be caught up in her business. Last thing I want is closer ties to somebody the Rebs might hang.

But the pop-pop of that auctioneer's hammer keeps knocking in my head. If I help Miss Bet, maybe it'll help another Liza some time. I guess Miss Bet and I should be fighting the Rebels, not each other, since they're the ones who keep hurting my people.

Wilson's feet are thumping the steps. Maybe he can help me think. Too many things have happened today—my head's feeling mixed up as turtle meat.

JANUARY 22, 1862

7:30 A.M.

Slept well, though a bit overly excited after last night's surprise. After dinner, Mother and I retired to the library. Somehow City Councillor Haskins has smuggled Northern newspapers into the city, and we were reading them when Nelson opened the double doors. "Somebody here to see you, Miss Bet," he announced with a smile.

Liza slipped from behind him and came in the room. She looked so pretty, so grown up! Her hair was parted in the middle, with braids neatly wound over each ear. A blue calico dress hugged her waist—she is lovely in blue, I must remember to tell her—and her face looked like an amber jewel. She nodded at Mother. "'Evening, Miz Van Lew. Can Miss Bet and I talk alone?" I was too surprised to move.

Mother yawned and decided it was bedtime. "Welcome back, child," she said, then left the two of us alone.

"What is it?" I asked. "Are you in trouble? Is Wilson ill?"

"No'm. It's time we get you back into Harwood Prison." Her voice was so determined. "I'll pretend to be your slave, and if they still won't let us in, we'll go directly to the Secretary of War for permission."

"What on earth?" When my eyebrows shot up, she laughed.

"That's right. Miss Clara says most men think with their stomachs. From what I hear of Benjamin's belly, Mama's custard could convince him to write a pass in a heartbeat."

I dare not tell Liza that going as my slave was Nelson's idea. We have agreed to protect her as long as possible, so the less she knows, the better. Nor will I tell her the custard bowl has a false bottom.

Into the prison the bowl will go, Northern newspapers hidden in the bottom for the officers. And out it will come, with notes on everything they can see from the third-floor windows . . . troop movements, activity at Tredegar Iron Works, the number of naval ships at Rockett's Landing, and instructions on how Union generals should prepare.

Thank God for Samuel Ruth, superintendent of the Richmond, Fredericksburg, and Potomac Railway. Haskins says he is a Unionist and will make sure the information reaches Washington by train.

It has just this moment occurred to me: Liza still has not apologized! And how does she know that Judah Benjamin has a potbelly?

◆—◆

JANUARY 24, 1862

A long, frustrating day. The "good Southern woman" ruse did not work. And when we went to the War Department, we were not allowed to see Benjamin, though his assistant Bledsoe spoke with us. I wish I had a photograph of Liza handing the bowl to him.

"Here you go, suh," she said with a slave's obedient smile. "This here custard's good for whut ails yuh. We'll leave it so's you and Mr. Benjamin can eat it fo' lunch."

But her act was all for nothing. Request was refused in this note delivered late today:

RICHMOND
JANUARY 24, 1862

My dear Miss Van Lew:

Judah Benjamin declined to act on your application and referred it to General Winder. He is the provost marshal of Confederate prisons. If I can see General Winder, I will try to get him to grant your request.

The custard was very nice, and many thanks to you. I borrowed

some cups from an eating house nearby, and bought some crackers.
So it was eaten in fine style.

TRULY YOURS
A. G. BLEDSOE
ASSISTANT SECRETARY OF WAR
CONFEDERATE STATES OF AMERICA

Well! They have passed us off to Winder. I will ask Caroline to make a fresh bowl of custard so Liza and I can tempt him tomorrow. Perhaps some flattery should be on the menu, too. I hear the man is quite vain about his silver hair.

LOCUST ALLEY

JANUARY 26, 1862

Walked over to the mansion this morning. Miss Bet showed me Bledsoe's note and told me to put my cloak back on. Said we were taking custard and compliments to Winder.

"Miss Bet," I announced, "I've got something else up my sleeve. Don't let's take the custard to Winder. Invite him here to your house, instead."

Then I whispered in her ear, telling every detail about Winder's visits to Miss Clara and how he pays her. Miss Bet looked so funny! Her mouth was round as a doughnut, but I knew better than to laugh. It surprised me, seeing her so embarrassed. Now that I'm married, I guess I'm older than Miss Bet in some ways.

Then she had a fit over Wilson and me living with a lady of the night. Same nagging, same ordering me around. Best to stay away from Miss Bet, since all we do is fight. Why is it so hard for older people to change?

2311 E. Grace Street

Richmond, Virginia

January 26, 1862

Dear Liza,

This is a note of thanks for your wise advice. I did just as you suggested. Instead of taking custard to the white-haired general, I invited him here for a private conversation. It would make a delightful write-up for the social column:

"The gracious hostess, Miss Elizabeth Van Lew, entertained General Winder at her home today. She spoke softly of Clara

Coleman as she offered ladyfingers and tea. Sadly, the general, on hearing the indecent details of his midnight wanderings, had a choking fit and was unable to partake."

After finding his voice, Winder asked for stationery and wrote a letter of permission on the spot. Now I can visit Harwood Prison often as I wish. Imagine—this war has turned me into a black-mailer. I rather like the idea.

However, I do not like the idea of my girl living in a brothel. I suppose it is no good to demand that you and Wilson live here, since it seems that you always get your way.

MISS BET

APRIL 7, 1862

Flyer posted on streetlamp in front of the house. They shall never get a morsel from this house.

ATTENTION, CITIZENS!

BODIES OF TROOPS

Will be passing through this city

TO-DAY, TO-NIGHT, AND TO-MORROW,

And the citizens are respectfully requested to send

COOKED PROVISIONS

To the store of L. ANTELOTTI, at the Central Railroad Depot.

JOSEPH MAYO,
Mayor of the City of Richmond.

Richmond, April 7, 1862.

MARCH 26, 1862

5 P.M.

The morning paper said Libby Warehouse is now the main prison for all Union officers. I went straight to Winder, but he refuses to allow any civilians in, even me.

Only six blocks away, hundreds of the country's finest men are in anguish. It might as well be six oceans, for all that I can help them or they can help me.

Friday, June 20, 1862

Mother and I put up currant jelly today. It is hot work but it passes the time. Nearly six weeks of intense anxiety have passed as we wait for General McClellan to seize Richmond from the Rebels. Nelson hears he is so short that his men call him "Little Mac." Apparently the general lacks courage as well as height.

Now he is only six miles to the east, and the Grays and the Blues have been lining up to fight for two days. Mother is certain of a Union victory. Weeks ago, she asked Caroline to prepare a room for the general. The chamber is quite attractive, with new floorcloths and sprigged curtains. We all call it "McClellan's Room" and are most anxious to receive him.

July 2, 1862

Scarcely a moment to write until today. McClellan finally took action last Thursday. I have just returned from Broad Street, where wounded men are arriving by the thousands. Only a handkerchief kept me from gagging. It is difficult to tell the age of the men, as their faces are blackened by gunpowder.

Most of the wasted wretches have lost an arm, a leg, or half a face. Many sat atop corpses in the wagons, too dazed to care. I looked through hundreds of carts for Jim Coffey's face—or worse, A. T.'s butchered body—until I could bear it no longer.

When the fighting began last week, Mother and I were so positive of a victory that Nelson drove us out to Mechanicsville Turnpike to welcome the Northern troops. For hours, thousands of soldiers veiled us in dust as they rushed to the battle on foaming horses. Cannons thundered in the distance, and Nelson said it was God roaring disapproval from the sky.

By the time the firing stopped at nine p.m., the turnpike was so crowded with ambulances that Nelson drove home by a different route. He fretted over Caroline the entire time. We were relieved to find her safe, though exhausted by fear—the fighting came so close that she could see shells exploding from the upstairs windows. She said each one jiggled the house like a giant shaking a baby doll.

And still the battles continue. . . . Wagons wind through the streets at all hours, bringing tens of thousands dead and wounded from Mechanicsville, White Oak Swamp, Malvern Hill. Ghastly losses on both sides, and for nothing! Lee is returning to the city. McClellan is withdrawing to the banks of the James River. Richmond remains in the hands of the Rebels.

I am bitter when I think of Richmond's Southern ladies. "Kill as many Yankees as you can for me!" they cried a year ago as they sent their sons and husbands to war. "Bring me a piece of Lincoln's ear!" I wonder if Confederate patriotism has worn thin, now that their men have returned in faceless pieces. Nelson has been down to Libby. He says the Confederates are cramming thousands of newly wounded Union officers inside a building meant to hold five hundred. Oh, what can I do for them?

2311 E. GRACE STREET
RICHMOND, VIRGINIA
JULY 5, 1862
7 P.M.

Dear Liza,

I must ask again for advice. City Councillor Haskins wants me to speak with a man whose name is Quaker. Haskins says he is a Scotsman who hates slavery of all kinds, and that he might be useful to the Union cause. But with the meeting only a day away, I am suddenly uneasy. What if Quaker is a Rebel?

My dear girl, you helped with the custard and shared the infor-mation on Winder. Can I count on you now? Would you ask Clara if she knows anything about Quaker? Please answer quickly. Nelson will wait for your reply.

Miss Bet

JULY 7, 1862

Mother always says I should meet new men. I am sure a midnight tryst in St. John's Cemetery is not what she had in mind.

When Quaker whispered to me from under the table-stone grave, his face was hidden in the blue-black night. He could have been anyone—a Rebel with a gun; a ne'er-do-well sleeping off too much drink. The Scottish accent reassured me, though, so I tucked in my skirts and crawled under the stone. "What is your full name?" I whispered.

"Quaker is all you need to know."

"How do you explain your loyalty to the Union?"

"I came to America to escape that fat English witch, Queen Victoria."

It sounded sincere enough—the English have kept generations of Scots in poverty. Then, as promised by Haskins, Quaker produced his escape map of Libby Prison. He thinks the men should dig a tunnel, and I agreed.

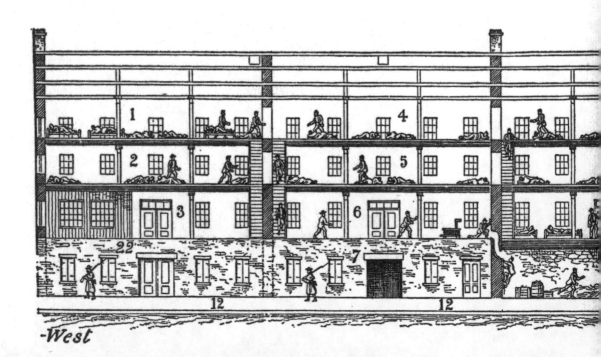

But today I wonder. Wouldn't escape by windows prove quicker? Somehow I must find out the height of the windows. Could prisoners lower themselves by rope? How long should the ropes be? How many would they need?

I asked Quaker about active loyalists in Richmond. He says there are over three hundred, and promises for safety's sake that the right hand never knows what the left is doing. He says I should be especially careful. The Van Lew name is floating around like pollen and sticking in every Rebel nose.

Richmond natives know my face and name too well, so a disguise would do no good. Perhaps I need another identity to do my work as a spy,   someone who is Bet but not Bet. There, I have written the word— "SPY!" This is what I am now, and it is best to face it.

For I will almost certainly be caught one day. Elizabeth Van Lew may not live to see the end of the war. God help me.

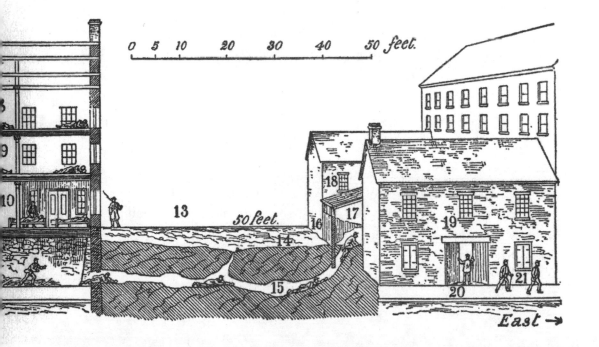

July 30, 1862

Weather hot as the devil's tongue. Wilson said he had to work extra long today, so I visited the kitchen house and walked in on some kind of sight. There was Miss Bet, standing in the middle of the floor, wearing a shabby one-piece skirt and a belted canvas jacket.

"What on earth, Miss Bet?" I asked. "Where'd you get those clothes?"

"Your father brought them in from the farm," she said. "And I am not Miss Bet today. Just an old crone without much sense." She made a crazy face and crossed her eyes.

Then Daddy brought out the buckskin leggings. When she tied them on, his knees crumpled and a big laugh burst out. Nothing would do but that he call Mama to see. I heard a sigh from upstairs. "Got the droops today, Nelson. Leave me be."

"Never mind that," he called up again. "Liza's here, and I know you want to meet this old farm woman who's come to see us. Bring down that faded poke bonnet—the one with the broad brim."

Mama trudged down the steps, fanning herself and grumbling about the heat. Even she had to smile when she tied the bonnet under Miss Bet's pointy chin. Still, Mama is no fool. "What you up to now, Miss Bet? Ain't nobody gonna know who you are in that getup. And if they do, they gonna think you loony."

"Just so," Miss Bet replied, and out she went, straight down the hill beside the house and toward the river. I waited a few minutes, then told Mama and Daddy I was going to follow her. Daddy had a fit and told me to stay put, but I was gone before he could stop me.

When Miss Bet reached Cary Street, she turned right and walked two blocks. Looked to me like she was heading straight for Libby Prison, and I was right.

I followed her around the back of the building, down the bare earth path that separates the back from the river canal. Every time she slowed down to look up at the windows on the third floor, I had to slow down, too. The whole thing made me jittery.

Just as I started to head back, Miss Bet turned the corner and wobbled her way to the front of the building. I slinked up to the edge and heard her talking to some guards. At first I couldn't make out the words, she seemed so confused.

"Mice blind three, mice blind three, run they how see, run they how see . . ." She was singing a nursery song—backwards!

When I poked my head around the corner, I saw Miss Bet's head flopping around on her neck. Every time she rolled her eyes, she sneaked a glance inside the windows. That woman is something else again. Not too many white women would make fools of themselves like she did today.

When she lurched away, a guard whispered, "Isn't that Elizabeth Van Lew?"

The other one laughed at her weaving backside. "It's her, all right—Betty Van Lew. From what I just seen, I'd call her Crazy Bet. A nigger lover, I hear. They say she was pretty once. Never married, though. Without a man around, a woman sure turns peculiar."

Well, Miss Bet always says men think a woman's mind is empty as a gourd. If they believe she's lost what few brains she has, they won't suspect her of . . . what *is* she up to now? Before I could put my thoughts together, the first guard spoke again.

"You ask me, a little too peculiar," he said. He looked at the upstairs windows. "If a Yankee sticks his head out, fire one warning shot. Keeps it out, shoot to kill. I'm going inside to make a report on this 'Crazy Bet' Van Lew."

I came on back to Miss Clara's, then. Goodness, it's hotter than fritters in this room. I'd tell Miss Bet about the report, but then she'd know I was spying on her.

Maybe I should talk to Daddy and let him tell her. Wait a minute! He brought her those clothes from her farm. Has she gotten him mixed up in her doings, too?

JULY 31, 1862

I regret that Nelson and I had our first argument this morning. When he insisted I ride to the farm with him, I thought it was to hear my report on Libby.

"Apparently the prisoners occupy only the top two floors," I said as he helped me up to the wagon seat, "though a good number seem to be dying in the infirmary on the first floor."

Nelson flicked the horse's reins, silent as a judge.

"There are windows on all four sides," I blathered on. "If each floor has two ropes for each side, the men will need sixteen ropes in all. I estimate they should be thirty to fifty-five feet in length. The longer ones will allow for the slope on the east end of the building. Nelson, perhaps you would ask John if there are extra ropes at one of the hardware stores and to hold them in reserve. Do not tell him what—"

Nelson interrupted. "Liza followed you yesterday," he said. "She thinks one of the guards has reported you."

"Oh, my dear Lord. Did they notice her? Did they connect her with me?"

"Don't know 'bout that. But I say it's time to tell her everything. The deeper you and I slide into this spy hole, the more she's in danger. She needs to know what's goin' on, so's she can watch out for herself."

"What a foolish girl she can be!" I said. "Nelson, you should share my spy activities with Caroline, but let's protect Liza as long as possible."

He strongly disagreed, and our ride ended in silence.

Yet the visitor this afternoon proves I am right. Around four o'clock, a gentleman knocked on our door. He claimed he had information from the Federal government that would be of great interest.

Though it was clearly a trap, Mother was hospitable as usual. I swear, if Satan came calling, she would offer him tea. We served Caroline's yellow lemon cake and kindly explained, no, we had no spare room for boarders; no, he could not sleep on the floor in the library; and yes, it was time that he be on his way.

We must be watchful—wise as serpents and harmless as doves, for truly the lions are seeking to devour us.

OCTOBER 9, 1862

Letter with flyer arrived today. Maybe Wilson will forget about it if I keep it here. . . .

DECEMBER 13, 1862

10 A.M.

Mrs. Taylor, Mother's old friend from Fredericksburg, called today. Poor soul. Though her husband and two sons are Confederate soldiers, she herself is a peaceable woman who cares nothing for slavery or states' rights.

She wept as she told us about the battle raging in F'burg this week. Union forces have turned her house into a hospital, and piles of amputated limbs are scattered across her yard. She fled here to be with her brother and fears the house may be gone when she returns.

The worst, she says, is not knowing where her husband is—his regiment has been fighting in Mississippi, and he is now missing in action. Do the men have any idea how their women suffer? I would give anything to stop the carnage. Anything!

2311 E. GRACE STREET

RICHMOND, VIRGINIA

DECEMBER 15, 1862

Dear Liza,

Sleep has not visited me this night, and since dawn is here, I can no longer postpone my painful task. I would have come in person, but from now on no one should see us together.

Dear girl, you have given help and advice when I needed it. Now I must ask for much more. Your parents and I discussed it in the parlor last night. Caroline was dead set against the idea, and I would rather die myself than ask you to risk your life. Your father finally convinced us both.

"Liza's ready," he said. "She's got common sense and a quick

memory. I've seen her look once at a page and remember everything on it. . . . She gets her commons from her mama, but that memory, it sure don't come from me."

The thing is, Liza, you are the only one who can carry out the plan. My friend, Mrs. Carrington, recently attended a Christmas gathering at the White House of the Confederacy. She reports that President Davis and his wife need an upstairs serving girl. Someone to mind their children, dust, lay the fires, that sort of thing. A slave, of course, is preferred.

I can easily arrange for you to have the job. It shall be done in secret, so no one in the White House will connect you to me. There are risks. You will have to be docile, a most unnatural state for you. Yet, all the while you must exercise your keen ability to remember everything you see and hear. But think of it! The information you could pass along, the lives you might save!

Nelson will return tomorrow for a reply.

HOPEFULLY,

MISS BET

LOCUST ALLEY

DECEMBER 28, 1862

Dear Miss Bet,

I've had to do some hard studying on your letter. For fifteen years you've been telling me what to do. Go to school in Philadelphia, Liza. Don't marry Wilson, Liza. Teach school, live in your mansion.

Now you want me to risk my life! Last night I was all set to write and tell you no, when Wilson walked through the door. He was stooped as an old man and sank in the straight-back chair. Didn't move, even after I rubbed his muscles with liniment. It hurt me so, seeing my Wilson pressed down like that.

Except for his sighs, the room was quiet, like a parlor when a body's laid out. Cold air came through a crack in the window, till the calico curtains breathed slow and shallow as a dying man.

"I'm tired of aiding the Confederates," Wilson finally said. "Sick of making killing machines at Tredegar."

I wanted to comfort him, but when he's feeling low, I've learned it's best just to listen.

"You know about that list of free Negroes at the courthouse. Since February, the Confederate army has been using it to draft free black men for pick-and-shovel labor. They've passed me over until now, but soon I'll be a marked man, too."

"Oh, God," I wailed.

"I'd rather die escaping to the North than spend one day digging trenches for the Rebs. I've got to get back to Philadelphia. That's where I can do the most for the Union and the poor slave."

"Make this war go away, Wilson!" I cried.

He pulled me down in his lap. "Shhh, dear wife, shhh," he whispered. "I've been thinking about that flyer I got in the mail a few months ago—the one from Mr. Epps, remember? I looked for it this morning but couldn't find it anywhere. Epps wrote a note on the back asking me to return to the city and organize a Negro regiment."

"Then I'll go with you," I said quickly.

"No! The Rebels are already so scared of free Negroes that they've cut off all our movement in Virginia. On January first, the Emancipation Proclamation takes effect. I suspect traveling will be even worse, then."

Wilson wrapped his arms around me. "I must get through Confederate lines and down to the Federal encampment at Fort Monroe. Two travelers would mean twice the danger. You're safer here with your parents and Miss Bet. You know she loves you like a daughter."

That's just the problem, I started to say, but he's right, Miss Bet. I guess that's why you turned to me for help. Now I'm turning to you.

Could you threaten Winder again? Make him write a pass so Wilson can get as far as Chaffin's Farm? From there, he could slip down the peninsula to the fort, then take a steamer to Philadelphia, and fight this war his own way.

I'd be lying if I said I wasn't scared to work at the White House. Miss Clara told me hundreds of suspected loyalists are in Richmond prisons, and nine of them are colored. You know as well as I do that three Union agents were kept in irons in Castle Thunder Prison for over a year. Starved first, then hanged.

I've never been to a hanging and don't want to start with my own. I don't want to choke until my tongue sticks out. Don't want to mess all over myself so people can see it drip to the ground. Don't want to die!

But Wilson needs me, and so do you. Get him through Rebel lines, Miss Bet, then I'll be your spy. If Daddy thinks I'm ready for it, then I guess I am.

LIZA

P.S. Don't tell Wilson about me and the White House. He's got enough on him. As far as my husband's concerned, I'm moving in with Mama and Daddy after he leaves.

1863–1865

Well, Polly, time came when Miss Bet and I did listen to each other. Had to. Because once we were Ellen Bee, we had no choice. And as it turned out, Ellen Bee was a better person than either of us on our own.

Didn't sleep well. Too much on my mind. In five months I'll be sixteen. What will this year bring for me, for Wilson?

Today is Freedom Day for slaves in Confederate states—at least the ones in South Carolina. Wilson says when Union troops took the S.C. Sea Islands in late sixty-one, plantation owners ran like rabbits, leaving the slaves behind. But until the Union takes back each Confederate state, nobody can force slaveholders to free one Negro soul.

James and Mary celebrated Emancipation Day by getting married at St. John's this morning. Mama and Daddy had a breakfast party for them, and Mama outdid herself. Daddy gave the dishes funny names—Hallelujah Ham, Glory Grits, and Elated Eggs—but I was too tired to laugh.

Miss Bet stopped by with a copy of the Emancipation Proclamation. The pages felt like angel wings when she put them in my hands. I tried reading, but my eyes started to swim, so Wilson took the sheets and recited each word loud and clear. After he finished, we said a prayer for those still legally enslaved in the territories and border states. Proclamation didn't free any of them.

Daddy tried to tease Miss Bet into dancing an Emancipation Jig, but she said she had business to do. "Nelson," she asked, "would you please bring the carriage around?" She worked her fingers into kid gloves and put on her cloak. I'd never breathe a word, but Miss Bet's too short for a cape. Makes her look like a pattypan squash.

"Stay awhile," Mama urged. "This is one day when we should all be together. Take us a rest from the war."

"I am going to the auction at the Ballard Hotel, Caroline. The Rebels are selling and hiring out slaves today, the same as they always do on January first. I plan to purchase at least one slave to set free."

"New Year's Day," Wilson said. "It's just another 'Heartbreak Day' as far as Negroes are concerned." He knelt by the woodstove and stoked the fire. "These seceshes need some black soldiers to teach them what the word 'freedom' means."

When he looked at me, his eyes were solemn and sad. Nobody spoke the words, but all our thoughts were running down the same river. Wilson will be with us just a few more days.

Miss Bet asked me to walk to the front of the house with her.

"Any news about that pass?" I whispered as we moved along the path.

"Winder has agreed to see me tomorrow. I will ask for permission to visit Chaffin's Farm. Tell Wilson to be ready—he will need a large blanket so he can hide in the back of the wagon."

Miss Bet squeezed my hand and asked me to climb in the carriage for a moment. She told me more about her Crazy Bet act, the man she had mentioned named Quaker, and the Libby escape plan. Then we talked woman to woman.

It took her a while to get it out, but she finally explained about Albert Terrell, or A. T., whom she loved years ago. Said she knew what it was like to lose somebody, and to be strong about Wilson, like she's been strong about Mr. A. T. I don't think I've ever felt so close to Miss Bet, and I told her so. She even let me touch the pendant watch he gave her so long ago. I've wondered why she always wears that chain around her neck.

Now I've got two heartaches, mine and hers. Poor Miss Bet. Well, at least she only lost her man. I'm about to lose Wilson *and* my freedom.

JANUARY 2, 1863

Purchased Louisa for one thousand dollars yesterday, then set her free. When I invited her to work here, she said she was leaving Virginia to find her child.

"I never had but one, missus," the pitiful mother cried, "and Mr. Smith sold him off to somebody in North Carolina."

2311 E. GRACE STREET

RICHMOND, VIRGINIA

WEDNESDAY, JANUARY 7, 1863

Dear Liza,

    Hide these directions in your album. This coming Saturday, Varina Davis is holding one of her famous levees at the White House of the Confederacy on Twelfth Street. (I do believe the woman would host a party at her own funeral.) She wants you to join the household that morning. Use the enclosed code to report military *information only. Hide it in your album, too, and keep the album in a safe place. I have folded mine into a square and slipped it in the back of my watch.*

    Quaker is posing as a baker. His shop is on North Fifth Street, and each morning he delivers tea cookies and scones to the carriage house at the White House. Arrange to be the one who meets him at the wagon.

    Look for a peach pit pin on his lapel. This is the Unionists' secret identification. The pins have a swinging three-leaf clover carved into them—if the clover is turned down, it is safe to speak.

I do not pretend to draw as well as you, my girl, but I have enclosed a sketch of the pin so you know what to look for.

If you have a military message, pass it to Quaker. He will slip it into a loaf of bread and make a bakery "delivery" to our kitchen house. Nelson will put messages inside the marble lion that sits on my hearth, and I will check it at night, when no one can see in the window. I am taking every precaution. Strange faces have been peering around the pillars on the rear portico. I suspect they are looking for evidence so they can put me in jail.

I will decode each message and give it to James, who will walk it to my farm in a false-soled leather shoe. From there, Bob or Oliver will take it to a hidden landing at the river. Bob is paying a young boy one thousand dollars of Van Lew money for each dispatch carried to Fort Monroe and delivered to a Union officer's hand.

I am not sure who will receive the messages or if they will believe the contents. Quaker has been trying to establish direct contact with Colonel Sharpe, the new head of Army Intelligence. Until then, we must hope that your information is put to good use by someone in charge.

To decode or write a message:
1. Each pair of numbers represents one letter of the alphabet.
2. To cipher a letter, find the first digit of the number in the column on the left. Find the second digit in the row on the bottom.
3. Look on the chart to see where the two meet. This box contains the alphabet letter.

One more thing. I told Quaker that coded military messages are not enough—I must be certain you are safe. He suggests we stay in touch through notes, but that using our real names is impossible, of course. He has taken the first letters of our first names, "L" and "B," to create a code name for the two of us.

So, my dear, we're both Ellen Bee now. Write notes to me when you can, addressed to Ellen Bee, and I shall do the same. Whenever possible, offer to run errands and slip by Clara's, whose code name is Lady.

Give her the note and pick up notes Crazy Bet has left for you. This should be safe enough . . . so far I have wandered the streets without suspicion, and everyone thinks I am a fool. Dear girl, this is all very complicated but necessary for your safety. Please exercise the greatest care. You are not of my body, but you are of my heart.

LOVE,
MISS BET

	1	**3**	**6**	**2**	**5**	**4**
6	*r*	*n*	*b*	*h*	*l*	*x*
3	*v*	*l*	*u*	*8*	*4*	*w*
1	*e*	*M*	*3*	*j*	*5*	*g*
5	*t*	*a*	*9*	*0*	*i*	*d*
2	*k*	*7*	*2*	*z*	*6*	*s*
4	*p*	*0*	*y*	*c*	*f*	*q*

Dear Ellen Bee,

I'll try to get this note over to Lady today, but it's hard as the dickens to find a safe time to write. I have to wait until the slaves are asleep or have left the kitchen house at dawn.

Arrived at six on Saturday morning, shaking from the snow. When I knocked on the basement door, a beautiful mulatto answered. She wore a black dress and white apron and looked like what Mama calls "a settled woman," with wavy hair slicked back and parted in the middle.

"'Morning, missus," I said. "I'm Liza, Mrs. Carrington's girl." I handed her the letter of introduction.

"Come in and wait here in the hall," she said. Thought I'd left the frost outside, but there was plenty hanging off her words.

Before long, she came back with Mrs. Varina Davis. Maybe the Confederate president's wife used to be a good-looking woman, but now she's fat and pale as a pig, except for those dark eyes. They look right through you. "I understand you love children," she said.

"Yes'm. Feels like a child myself most times." I giggled and cast down my eyes.

Varina turned to her maid. "Show Liza her place in the quarters and find her an apron. Then take her up to the nursery."

I followed the maid, dragging my gunnysack behind me. The kitchen house is a few yards behind the White House and has no windows. Except for a few live coals glowing in the fireplace, it was plenty dark. When I looked around for beds, all I saw was one straw tick pallet on the floor.

"Sadie and Lucy sleep in the loft," the maid said. "But there's no room for you up there. You'll sleep down here by the fireplace."

"Yes'm." I dropped my sack and my dignity on the plank floor. "Where yo' pallet?" I asked sweetly. I knew good and well she slept in the main house, but I figured it was better to act stupid.

She sucked herself up like a princess. "I'm Miz Varina's personal *servant*. I sleep in her room." Knew right off I couldn't trust this one as far as I could throw her.

Anyway, Ellen Bee, at least I get to sleep by the fire. I need the light to write by. And I spotted a loose floor plank next to the hearth. I'm hiding my album under it, along with any notes I get from you.

Now for the mansion. It's bigger than it looks. Three floors and a basement. All the rooms on the first level, except the state dining room, are alike. Wine-colored walls. Wine-colored upholstery. Wine-colored carpet and drapes. Good Lord, in the Confederate White House, it's nighttime all day long.

Princess led me up a narrow back staircase to the nursery, sitting room, and Jefferson Davis's office. We peeked in the nursery. Jeff Jr., eight-year-old Maggie, little Joe, baby Billy—all sound asleep—and after looking around, I prayed real hard they like long *naps*. Cribs and beds in every corner, toys all over the floor. I could tell this bunch is going to be a handful.

"Bedrooms are on the third floor," Princess said, "though you needn't concern yourself with them. This floor is your responsibility, including Mr. Davis's office. Dust his desk and bookshelves, empty the waste can, lay the fire. But stay out of his way—he has important visitors, you know."

During all this, I tried to look as eager as a pup with a bone.

"Mr. Davis is resting upstairs with a sick headache," she went on. "When he takes a bad spell, he works at home instead of the Capitol."

We walked into the office, and Ellen Bee, you won't believe what I saw! A sampler over the mantel, embroidered by Mrs. Davis. "Thy Will Be Done," it says. Sure sounded familiar.

Jeff Davis must have been working on something all night. Mountains of paper were piled on the mahogany desk and in his leather chair. I don't know when I can get back in there, but I'll try to do it soon.

Some good luck this morning. Princess told me to meet the bakery wagon starting today, so I stood at the back gate and waited until a cigarette stub of a man rode up in his wagon. Just like you said, Quaker had a peach pit pin on his jacket. He turned the clover down and handed me a package of tea cookies wrapped in brown paper. "Be careful, lassie," he said real low.

"Yassuh."

Quaker turned to the young Negro holding the reins. "This is Chris. He's my driver and a hard worker. Trustworthy, if you know what I mean."

I smiled at Chris. Made me feel better to see a colored man with Quaker. Ellen, you never told me how crabby the Scotsman looks. Those hooded eyes and bad teeth! Or maybe it's the accent. When he talks, sounds like gravel is rolling under his tongue.

Guess I better learn to like him. Except for my album, Quaker is all I got.

FEBRUARY 3, 1863

Message in the marble lion tonight!

33 // //' 24   13 // 63   63 // 53 6/   45' 66 14
24 5/ 53 6/ 3/ 55 63 14.
5/ 62 //   6/ 53 5/ 24   53 6/ //   // 53 5/ 55 63 14
6/ 53 5/ 24.
13 43 24 5/   62 53 3/ //   63 43   24 62 43 // 24
43 6/   42 43 53 5/ 24.

SHOES OR COATS.

LEE'S MEN NEAR F'BG STARVING. THE RATS ARE EATING RATS. MOST HAVE NO

This spy business is looking harder than I thought. Princess is Varina's pet watchdog and guards my every move. When I slipped my first message to Quaker last week, she stood watching from the back door. Sugar! I was so scared!

And I think she hates me because the children like me better. Maggie came right out and told me so. We were in the nursery, sitting on the floor, and I was showing her how to make paper dolls. They reminded me of Sarah—I wonder if my old friend is safe.

"You're fun, Liza," Maggie said. "Princess is too starchy. Besides, she carries tales on you. Last night she told Mama you spend more time playing with Joe and me than doing your work. But I told Mother you are the kindest nursemaid I've ever had."

Then that precious Maggie gave me a hug and the paper doll. She said to keep it so I won't forget her.

I play a lot of checkers with Joe, but I don't spend much time with Jeff, Jr. He's too busy playing soldiers with his gang. Every day the so-called Gentlemen's sons throw stones and bats down at the "Hill Cats," the Butcher Town boys who live by the river. Seems to me that Jeff, Jr., has entirely too much freedom for a six-year-old.

Poor little Joe begs to go along, though his big brother runs out of the house without him every time. So I tied Jeff, Jr.'s, rump in a knot. I told him, "If you don't take your brother along, I'll tell the Hill Cats that you take dance lessons!"

Two-year-old Billy loves how I make his spinning top dance across the carpet. He waddles around and smacks it with his chubby little hands, and

I plant a kiss on his cheek every time. Sometimes I have to remind myself whose children these are.

◆—◆

FEBRUARY 14, 1863

Valentine's Day. I put little Billy goat down for a nap, then went over to see Lady. It's not easy to get away. Today I told Princess that Sadie wanted me to borrow a needle from Mrs. Carrington. She didn't look too happy with the answer, but I slipped out, anyway.

Lady gave me a card and letter from Wilson! She said it came on a flag of truce boat and that a paid messenger delivered it to Grace Street last night. Crazy Bet brought it over this morning. I've read it ten times!

I don't know what I'd do if I couldn't write in this album or keep my letters here. Thank goodness for the loose plank by the fireplace. Sadie is old and can't see well, so she's never noticed it. And Lucy's tongue keeps her too busy. That girl sure loves to talk.

Dear Liza,

I wish you were here beside me, though this canvas tent and dirt floor might not be to your liking. How I miss you and our talks. I've made a decision, and I hope you'll think it's a wise one. I'm going to stay on at Fort Monroe, for I believe I can do more good here than in Philadelphia.

I've been working for the quartermaster, issuing supplies to the soldiers. At night, I teach former slaves to read. So many find refuge in this place that they call it "Freedom Fort."

The colored men work in the supply and engineering departments or build fortifications. Some act as personal servants to the officers. A few fish and dig oysters for a living. The women cook, wash, and iron for the soldiers and raise small gardens to feed their families.

Liza, if you could see our people pulling together, you would understand why I can't leave them. If we Negroes are ever allowed to fight, I'll be proud to serve alongside the men I've met here. Please know that I love you, and write as often as you can.

YOUR VALENTINE ALWAYS,

WILSON

APRIL 3, 1863
11:30 P.M.

Nothing is safe in this prison camp! Sadie was poking a log in the fireplace tonight and stubbed her toe on the loose board.

"Need to do somtin' 'bout that plank," she said. I stopped breathing when she leaned over. Thought for sure she'd lift the board and see my album, but she just wanted to rub her toe.

"This ol' foot hurts enough already. Don't need nutin' to make it worser. Liza, you remind me to get one of them boys out here to nail it down. Tell me at first light, or I'll forget for sure."

"Yes'm," I said, knowing I'd do no such thing. If that board gets nailed down, they might as well make me a coffin and drive nails in it, too.

MAY 10, 1863

Stonewall Jackson is gone! The Confederates' greatest hero, shot accidentally by one of his own men last week at the Battle of Chancellorsville. He died of pneumonia after they amputated his arm. I wanted to celebrate, but Mother said it would be un-Christian.

There were hideous losses on both sides at Chancellorsville. Lee, thirteen thousand casualties. Hooker, seventeen thousand. Pope, McClellan, Burnside, now Hooker. When will Lincoln find a Union general who can fight the Confederates? Despite the dreadful scourge of war, I am awed by the Rebels' wild courage. Time and again they push the Union back, though their numbers are less, their casualties often higher. The Confederacy has set new standards for determination. I only wish slavery were not at the heart of it all.

◆▬◆

MAY 11, 1863

3:30 P.M.

Jackson's body arriving by train today for state funeral tomorrow. Church bells were to toll from ten this morning until the train arrived at noon, but oh, dear me, the train is late!

For over five hours we have been victims of the steeple man at St. John's across the street. Mother finally stuffed her ears with cotton lint and settled into Papa's sofa with her sewing basket. She is making socks for the Libby men. Somehow I will get them inside—I think Quaker knows a particularly greedy guard.

All shops shut down for the funeral. John closed at eleven and stopped by with wife, Mary, and little Eliza.

"No need to excite suspicion," he said loudly over the clanging, "though we cannot afford to lose still more business, even for a day. Not with flour at forty dollars a barrel and potatoes twelve dollars a pound. Of course, we could always exchange our American dollars for worthless Rebel bills. They shall be worth a fortune one day!"

He pulled a Confederate note from his pocket.

"Here you are, Sister," he joked, "buy yourself a shoelace."

I smiled, grateful that John is too good-natured to say what we all know—the Van Lew fortune is slowly bleeding away. He did not complain when I bought Louisa for one thousand dollars last January, but he must not learn about the thousands I pay for bribes. It would only alarm him.

I asked if he still had lengths of rope hidden at the store. He assured me they were packed safely away. Dear, good John—he never asks what the ropes are for, or when they will be needed. I myself don't know when the escape will take place. Quaker thinks this coming winter would be best. A dark, rainy night, when damp cold would make the guards careless.

After lunch, Mother suggested we all move to the veranda and smell the Virginia spring. Will heaven be as charming as the south in May? If not, I do not care to go.

Nine-year-old Eliza was a great distraction from the bells. Mother chased her around the rockers and called her a darling pet plaything, until the poor child looked almost smothered.

For a moment, I was chilled by thoughts of my own girl's fate. While I sit safely here on my high hill, she is in the belly of the beast. Not a word from her in months—is she safe? Is there nothing useful she can pass on?

MAY 17, 1863

31 53 41 55 42 21 11 54 42 33 11 53 63

43 45 45 43 43 54.

33 11 11 41 33 53 63 24 51 43 55 63 31 53 54 11

41 53 24 43 62 43 61 24 11 24 53 63 54

13 11 63 42 53 63 11 53 51.

62 53 24 23 15, 52 52 52 51 61 43 43 41 24.

VA PICKED CLEAN OF FOOD. LEE PLANS TO INVADE PA SO HORSES AND MEN CAN EAT. HAS 75,000 TROOPS.

JULY 4, 1863

God is smiling on the Union. Maybe all this spying is finally making a difference. Lee's plan was a disaster. Great Union victory at Gettysburg, Pennsylvania. Vicksburg, Mississippi, and Chattanooga, Tennessee, have fallen, too.

The mood here is dark as dirt. Some Southern sympathizer smuggled in a photograph of a Yankee amputation at Gettysburg. I saw it on Davis's desk and figured he wouldn't notice if I took it for my album.

It's too grisly to think about. This fellow's losing his leg, but I hear that men in the trenches usually lose a finger or hand. Soon as they lift the ramrod to push powder down in the barrel, snipers take a shot. Lose a leg, at least you walk with a crutch. Lose a hand, nothing but a stump left, tied in an empty sleeve. Please, God. Let Wilson stay safely at Fort Monroe and not lose any parts at all.

Should I tell Miss Bet that Mr. A. T.'s name is on the list of missing at Gettysburg? Means he's either dead or in prison. Probably dead. From what I hear about Federal prisons, they're death factories just like ours. Mercy, no. This is one secret message that's staying with me.

FORT MONROE, VIRGINIA
DECEMBER 20, 1863

Dear Wife,

General Butler has returned from New Orleans and is now head of Fort Monroe. He has set up a secret mail service for the troops, so this letter should arrive safely at Miss Bet's by Christmas Eve.

I have proud news! The U.S. Colored Troops, First Regiment, was raised by the general at Fort Hamilton yesterday, and I've joined. Now the colored men wear the same blue uniform as the white troops but, like the white soldiers, we must be prepared to go where the army sends us.

I wish you could see us. With our new canteens, shot bags, and rifles, we are a good-looking lot. Hope you are enjoying the season with your parents and Miss Bet. Give them all my best, and have a Merry Christmas in the kitchen house, dear one. It may be a while before you hear from me, but remember, we will be together again.

YOUR AFFECTIONATE HUSBAND,

WILSON

"The Eagle shall bear the Rattlesnake in his beak and rend him with his talons."

THE WAR FOR THE UNION

Mary Elizabeth Bowser
2311 East Grace Street
Richmond, Virginia

Christmas. But there's nothing to celebrate. Lord knows where they've sent Wilson by now. What if he's captured? Confederates send black soldiers into slavery, when they don't shoot them on the spot.

I'm missing my husband so. Wish I could tell him that President Davis is crumbling like a stale cookie. Somebody shot at him while he was out riding his horse. Old Jeff claims he wasn't afraid, but he's got plenty of enemies, even in the Confederacy. Some of the servants say he's tried to poison himself twice.

It's late. I should go to sleep, but this is the first quiet time I've had all day. Sadie and Lucy are still in the main house, helping the wilted magnolia blossoms that Mrs. Davis invited over. They're all making dolls and ornaments for the Episcopal orphanage. I figure I've worked enough for one day.

Seen enough, too. After supper Mrs. Davis and her guests played with a windup toy . . . a little Negro boy that dances the buck and wing. Everybody passed it around and had a good laugh. Then Mrs. Davis gave each servant a handkerchief. Lucy hopped around like a fool." Oh, missus, this the most pretty present I's ever got!" she cooed.

Well, I guess it's like Mama says . . . if Lucy knew better, she'd do better. When nobody was looking, I spit in my hankie. Now I'm scared to throw it away. Princess might find it and wonder why.

DECEMBER 25, 1863

11 P.M.

Crazy Bet wandered over to Clara's this morning and picked up a note from Ellen Bee. It was so brief, so sad. My girl is afraid for Wilson, and I am afraid for her. Yet neither of us can give in to fear, not until the war is over.

After a somber dinner tonight, Mother and I exchanged presents in the drawing room. A crocheted sewing bag for her, sheet music to "Lorena" for me. I pretended pleasure, but the song is breaking war-weary hearts across the country. God knows, I need nothing else to break mine, not with Liza living in the lion's den.

I hear firecrackers in the streets. Christmas parties are underway—nothing stops Richmond when it wants to amuse itself. I wonder where they find the money for eggnog, with milk at twenty dollars a gallon? Bribes, black market, theft—the city is as rotten as wormy wood.

DECEMBER 26, 1863

Hard freeze last night. Even a long flannel gown and the heated bricks Mary wrapped in the quilt did not warm me. The gas streetlights were out of order again, so Quaker slipped through dark alleys and paid a visit.

He brought a report from Libby. Two white blacksmiths and five Negro helpers have put iron bars on every window. He says our plan to use ropes must be changed.

He also brought news of the men at Belle Isle. Less than a mile away from this mansion, six thousand prisoners are sleeping in sandy holes soaked with bloody diarrhea and dysentery. The lucky ones have packing boxes or tattered tents as cover. Most have none at all.

Quaker says the men are dying faster than diseased sheep. He believes the situation is critical, and Richmond must be captured before more die. He thinks I should try to establish direct contact with General Butler.

But would Butler trust me, a Southern woman? Oh, the irritation of it—to be under suspicion from both sides, North and South! Southerners think I am a Yankee. A Yankee general will assume I am a Rebel.

Must I pay such a heavy price for my beliefs—is it not enough that I sleep alone? Perhaps I shall contact Butler by sending a letter and fresh flowers via Dr. McCaw. The general might believe a man.

Quaker did bring some cheerful news. The Libby guard whom he bribes says the prisoners held a minstrel show last night. Because they are officers, Winder gave them permission to use an old press they found in a storeroom. Quaker gave me this copy of the program, and as I look at it, I marvel at their strength of spirit.

THE
LIBBY PRISON
MINSTRELS!

MANAGER,	– –	LT. G. W. CHANDLER.
TREASURER,	- -	CAPT. H. W. SAWYER.
COSTUMER,	- - -	LT. J. P. JONES.
SCENIC ARTIST,	- . -	LT. FENTRESS.
CAPTAIN OF THE SUPERS,	- -	LT. BRISTOW,

THURSDAY EVENING, DEC. 24th, 1863.

PROGRAMME.

PART FIRST.

OVERTURE—"Norma"................................TROUPE.
OPENING CHORUS—"Ernani"...................TROUPE.
SONG—Who will care for Mother now   Capt. SCHELL.
SONG—Grafted in the Army.............Lieut. KENDALL.
SONG—When the Bloom is on the Rye Adjt LOMBARD
SONG—Barn-yard Imitations...............Capt. MASS.
SONG—Do they think of me at Home...... Adjt. JONES.
CHORUS—Phantom..............................TROUPE.

PART SECOND.

Duet—Violin and Flute—Serenade from "Lucia,"
                    Lieuts. Chandler and Rockwell
Song and Dance—"Root Hog or Die,..............Capt. Mass
Banjo Solo...Lieut. Thomas
Duet—Dying Girl's Last Request, Adjt. Lombard & Jones
Magic Violin..............Capts. Mass, Chandler and Kendall
Song—My Father's Custom.................Lieut. McCaulley
Clog Dance...Lieut. Ryan

RIVAL LOVERS.

JOE SKIMMERHORN...........................Capt. MASS
GEORGE IVERSON........................Lt. RANDOLPH

Some prisoners sent gifts to me through Quaker. A pair of cunning rings carved from dog bone (gracious heaven, are they giving them hound meat to eat now?) and a carved wooden book. My initials are one side, the words "a friend in need" on the other. It must have taken days to whittle the trinkets. I suppose it is a diversion for the men . . . something to do besides capture the regiments of lice that march through their filthy clothes.

How the months limp by. Where is the war's quick end that we had hoped for after Gettysburg?

—◆—

JANUARY 19, 1864

Letter brought by Dr. McCaw this afternoon. I now have personal access to Butler. What a clever general—his real message, as the doctor explained, is written between the lines in lemon juice. I waited until everyone was in bed, then applied candle heat to read it.

Norfolk, Virginia
January 18, 1864

MY DEAR AUNT:
My Dear Miss Van Lew:
I suppose you have been wondering why your nephew has not
The doctor who came through and spoke to me of the bouquet
written before, but we have been uncertain whether we should be
said that you would be willing to aid the Union cause by
able to send a letter. The Yankees steal all the letters that
furnishing me with information if I would devise a
have any money in them through flag of truce, so that we thought
means. You can write through flag of truce, directed to James
we would wait until we got a safe chance. I am glad to write
Jones, Norfolk, the letter being written as this is, in
that Mary is a great deal better. Her cough has improved, and

lemon juice, and decoded by application of heat, as directed by

the doctor has some hope. Your niece Jennie sends love, and

the messenger who brings this. I cannot refrain from saying to

says she wishes you could come North, but I suppose that is

you that although personally unknown, how much I am rejoiced to

impossible. Mother tells me to say that she has given up all

hear of the strong feeling for Union that exists in your own

hopes of meeting you, until we all meet in heaven.

breast and among some of the ladies of Richmond. I have the honor to be

Yours affectionately,

Very respectfully your obedient servant,

James Jones

Benjamin F. Butler

JANUARY 20, 1864

Feels like a train's coming and I'm tied to the track. This morning, I found a crumpled dispatch about numbers of Confederate troops in President Davis's trash. It seemed like something Ellen Bee should know, so I quietly closed the door. But I barely had time to memorize the words before I heard a rustle behind me.

Princess must be a ghost. I swear, she came right through that door without even opening it. She didn't say anything. Didn't have to. Her dark eyes cut me up like pork in a sausage grinder.

If she suspects I can read, I'll soon be wearing a rope necklace. And Lucy's full of gossip today. She says two of the downstairs slaves are planning to set fire to the White House. Oh, glory—I've got to get out of here!

NOTE FROM QUAKER IN THE LION TODAY:

Dear Ellen Bee:

A reliable friend has news from the boardinghouse near your mansion . . . the one on the river canal. The fellows who room there are feeling **blue**. *They are anxious to escape from these* **gray** *winter skies.*

He says the boys are planning an evening social. They will not be decorating the windows with ropes but are digging in the garden instead. They use tin cups from dark until daylight and have made great progress.

The party will be held one evening soon. Some plan to stop by your house after it begins. Could you fix up an extra room in your attic . . . perhaps the large space under your eaves?

Another thing, and this is important! This morning your namesake told me that servants are not to be trusted. Two black rascals who live at her house set fire to the basement last night, then ran off with silver tableware. The family slaves are closely watching the hired ones.

Our Ellen says she is sick with fear. She wants to leave her post and find her husband. I convinced her that friends should stay together in these troublesome times, but I don't know how much longer she'll be with us.

QUAKER

JANUARY 24, 1864

33 11 11' 24 53 61 13 46 43 63 33 46

26 15, 52 52 52 24 41 61 11 53 54 51 62 55 63

53 24 24 43 36 41. 65 15, 52 52 52 13 43 61 11

55 63 41 11 51 11 61 24 66 36 61 14.

Don't care if it's not in code. The pot handle's getting too hot to hold. I need to leave!

◆━◆

JANUARY 24, 1864

Dear Ellen Bee:

Do not abandon me now—how can I do this alone?! I've written to General Butler with your latest figures, and am paying a courier one thousand dollars in gold to put it in his hands. With Lee's men spread so thin, surely this is the best time to mount a raid, free the prisoners, and seize the city.

Listen carefully, Ellen. If Butler follows my advice and Richmond falls, come directly to the mansion. Your parents are wild with worry. They want you home as soon as your job is done. So do I.

Meanwhile, I hope you are getting enough to eat. Alas for the suffering of the very poor! Women are begging for bread with tears in their eyes. A week ago Thursday, I went through the city for a meal and could not get a particle anywhere.

I tried to get rice but could not. We bought one hundred pounds for fifty dollars a few days later. This Friday we bought a bushel of meal for $225 per barrel. There is a starvation panic upon the people.

I can no longer go to church. I went last Sunday to a Friends' Meeting, and heard the preacher pray, "God, bless the Confederate Congress." This I could not do.

◆━◆

LEE'S ARMY ONLY 25,000 BUT SPREAD THIN AS SOUP. 15,000 MORE IN PETERSBURG.

Dear Ellen Bee,

You're worse than a sneeze—once you get started, can't anything stop you. I've been doing some thinking about why I stay here. Is it because you love me? Well, every day brings me one step closer to hanging, so maybe your love's not the right kind.

Yes, I'll stay, but only for Wilson's sake and the chance that Ellen Bee might save his life one day. But I'm not coming back to the mansion. One generation of my family working in your house is enough. I sometimes question why Mama and Daddy have stayed on. Do they think they're better off with you? Or do they think they owe you for setting them free?

Make no mistake, if Richmond falls, I plan to join my husband. I might have to be a camp follower—cook over an open fire, sleep outside. As long as I'm near him, I don't care.

Camp life couldn't be any worse than here. Ever since Jim Pemberton and Betsy set fire to the basement, Princess rides my skirt tail. I can't even go to the privy without her hanging around the door. She could be hiding in the bushes outside right now, watching me write this note!

These are hard words, but please understand . . . I'm tired of walking the chalk around here. Don't know how much longer I can act in this play.

FEBRUARY 9, 1864

5 P.M.

Dear Ellen Bee,

No one, not even an eighteen-year-old, can see into anyone else's heart. Your parents and I share a great affection. They have been free to leave for twelve years, and when this brutal conflict is over, perhaps they will. Meanwhile, they have chosen to stay and help win the war. I pray you will continue to do the same.

As to Wilson, even if you knew his whereabouts, we could care for you much better here. We have all become quite handy at keeping the Rebels at bay. Five soldiers pounded on the door this afternoon. I must admit to breaking out in a perfect sweat. Quickly I mussed my hair, yanked Caroline's apron from her, and tied it backwards on myself. Mother answered the door and graciously offered cake and wine to our "guests." Then silly old Crazy Bet giggled as she led them through the house—even up to the attic.

They searched through old clothes and dusty trunks, but they never noticed the washstand Nelson had placed against the wall. It hides a trapdoor to our secret space. I managed not to bite my nails, but only because your father was so calm.

Painful news. My brother John has been conscripted into the Confederate army. He is ordered to report to Camp Lee today.

CHESTERFIELD COUNTY, TEN MILES FROM RICHMOND

FEBRUARY 9, 1864

Eleven-thirty by my watch. I am still waiting for my hostess to stop puffing on her pipe and go to sleep. She and her husband have been hiding John all day. I should feel grateful, but I am too weary.

Brother deserted today and is in great peril. He made his way here to the safe house, and the farmer immediately came to fetch me. I threw on my crazy outfit, left hurried instructions for the servants, and climbed in the wagon for a two-hour ride on back roads.

The bleak countryside dismayed me. Such desolation of ruined fields, burned houses, and broken trees, though I found some comfort in the bare winter beauty. Here a spiral of squirrels on an oak tree, there a heart-shaped flock of birds. I try to understand Southerners who would die for this graceful land. That if they are false to the Union, they believe they are true to their state.

With this jumble of thoughts, the trip went quickly enough. We reached the cabin at dusk, enough time to spend a few hours with John before retiring. He is sharing the farmer's bed downstairs. I will be sleeping with the wife. I do not look forward to it—I am certain she will snore.

◆—◆

FEBRUARY 10, 1 P.M.

Nelson arrived at the cabin this morning, bringing food from Caroline. Not much, but enough to get Brother through the lines. John and I went out to meet the wagon.

"Morning, missus," Nelson said, climbing down with a basket in his hand. "I brung more than ham biscuits. Great trouble and excitement at your house last night. Around seven, some skinny, dirty men knocked on the side door."

"Rebels looking for me!" Brother exclaimed.

"That's what I thought, Mr. John. They asked for somebody named Colonel Streight. Said they was to meet him at Miss Bet's place. I wouldn't let 'em in. They looked like bad apples to me."

It is dismal news, but I cannot fault Nelson. We have planned the Libby Prison escape for two years. How could we know it would happen last night!

"Colonel Streight is a Union officer," I said, "and a Libby prisoner. Where did the men go?"

"Some ran away, but a big bunch moved over to the wall between St. John's and the street and hunkered down awhile. Guess they were waiting for you to come home."

"Oh, good Lord," I moaned. "For three weeks we've had blankets over the gable windows . . . kept the gas burning low . . . prepared beds . . ."

John and I quickly decided that with Rebels hunting for escapees, crossing the lines would be too risky. He has returned with me to the mansion and is now hiding in the attic.

I will write to Winder—tell him John has deserted and demand that he write a letter of medical leave for Brother. But first I must visit the other safe houses and look for Colonel Streight.

Mother just came in to say mounted cavalry are roaming the streets three abreast. They are searching for the Libby men with a vicious bloodhound they call Hero.

"It does not matter," I replied. "They will let Crazy Bet pass. They always do."

FEBRUARY 28, 1864

66 55 14 46 53 63 21 11 11 61 53 55 54
42 52 13 55 63 14. 61 11 66 11 33 24 41 46
51 43 33 54 12 11 45 45.

BIG YANKEE RAID COMING. REBEL SPY TOLD JEFF.

127

TUESDAY, MARCH 2, 1864

Liza was right. Great panic in the city. Four thousand Federal cavalry are closing in.

Nelson brings word from the streets. The troops are in Goochland, one county to the west, and alarm bells rang for Home Guard volunteers all day. Able-bodied men (can there be any left?) answered the call, including boys under eighteen and the walking wounded.

Quaker thinks Lincoln himself is behind the raid—that my letters with Liza's information reached Washington. I am so proud of Ellen Bee! Without her January message, Lincoln would not know Lee's army is scattered across Virginia, leaving Richmond open to attack.

Meanwhile, Mother and I sit and stare at each other. We must stay busy—I shall light the lamp and pay some bills, and she can stitch up more miniature flags. Hundreds of Unionists here offer to buy them, but she will not hear a word of it and gives them away.

The "medical leave" that Winder granted to John has ended. He was approved for duty yesterday—Confederate army, Eighteenth Regiment, Company C—but he swears he will desert again at the first possible chance. Mother begged his wife, Mary, to bring little Eliza and stay with us, but Mary said she would miss John less if she slept in their own bed.

I hear frozen snow clicking on the roof—is Brother warm enough?

❖

THURSDAY, MARCH 4, 1864

A fitful night, with dreams of John lying frozen in the fields. Awoke to the news that the entire Union raid was a failure. Loyalists in Richmond are heartbroken. Lohmann says the leader of the raid, Colonel Dahlgren, was a family friend of President Lincoln, a son of Admiral Dahlgren, and the youngest colonel in the army.

But the fair Dahlgren was ambushed Tuesday night by Confederate Home Guard and shot in the back. To think that only seven months ago he was near death after losing a leg at Gettysburg, yet he risked this daring assault!

Papers were found in the colonel's jacket—complete plans to free the Union prisoners, capture Davis, and torch the city. Richmond is all agog. They wonder how Yankees could dare to take the president. What do they think war is, a debutante ball?

Poor Dahlgren's body is lying in a boxcar at the York River Depot, and his wooden leg is on display in a shop window. I went down to see what I could do but left immediately. The oglers disgust me. Davis refuses to return Dahlgren to his father in Massachusetts, and the newspapers say he'll have a dog's burial in a hidden place. The shame of it!

Am in much low depression of spirit. If not for Ellen Bee's message to Butler, would Dahlgren be alive tonight?

MARCH 5, 1864

54 53 62 33 14 61 11 63 51 43 66 11 66 36 61 55 11 54
43 53 21 34 43 43 54 51 43 63 55 14 62 51.

APRIL 2, 1864

Quaker is putting the rest of the Van Lew money to good use. For weeks he has bribed some of the poorest women in town to organize a food protest. This morning, with pistols in hand, two hungry women led hundreds of others to the government commissary this morning. They left carrying flour, hams, and shoes . . . whatever their emaciated arms could hold.

After alarm bells sounded, James went down to the Capitol and watched the scene.

"When thieves and looters joined the women," he reported a few hours later, "all hell broke loose. The mob smashed shop windows with axes and stole hats, tools, rolls of silk. Then the Big Hats showed up.

"The Governor told firemen to turn water hoses on the crowd . . . the Mayor read the Riot Act . . . Jeff Davis came and stood on a wagon. He offered to share his last loaf of bread, emptied his pockets of money, and threw it at the mob."

"We do not wish to injure anyone," Davis said, "but this lawlessness must stop. I will give you five minutes to disperse, otherwise you will be fired upon."

James said the crowd slowly disappeared, but I think the women will be back. Men should never underestimate the power of mothers with hungry children. Babies cannot eat paper bills—even Confederate ones.

We have fasted all day in honor of the starving poor, though I told Mother she must have some dinner. An empty stomach has given me a clear head, and I have now a plan for poor Dahlgren's remains. Thanks to Liza's last message, it should work.

When the Rebels buried the colonel, Chris dressed up as a cemetery worker and hid behind a tree. He knows the exact location of the grave, and on the next cloudy night, he and Mr. Lohmann will dig up the body. They can rebury it in a secret place until Admiral Dahlgren can bring it home. Young Dahlgren lived his brief life in such danger. At least I can make sure he is safe in death.

Caroline is ringing the bell for dinner. Broth and biscuits, she said. Mother needs something more substantial—she is altogether too thin. Oh, for a thick slice of roast beef!

Sadie and Lucy are snoring upstairs, thank goodness. Just enough firelight left for writing.

I made my acquaintance with the dead last night. Quaker's been out of town on a mission, so Chris made the delivery alone yesterday morning. He said Miss Bet had organized a party to dig up Dahlgren, and that she might join them sometime during the night.

Chris didn't like the idea, but I said I was going, too. Figured this was my chance to convince Miss Bet I'm not coming back to the mansion, no matter what. My chance to tell her she reminds me of that William Garrison and his newspapers. For Garrison and Miss Bet, free Negroes are dandy until they start liberating themselves.

At bedtime I waited for Lucy and Sadie to fall asleep, then I crept out and ran all the way to the bakery. Chris headed the wagon to Oakwood Cemetery, where we met Mr. Lohmann near the back entrance.

I've never been in a cemetery at night and don't believe I'll go again. The dark was thick as syrup. Shrouds of rainy mist hung over the tombstones. I picked up a shovel and offered to dig, just to take my mind off ghosts and other things it's better not to think about.

"Stand back, girl," Mr. Lohmann said in a chewy German accent. "This is man's work."

The grave was shallow, and before long he reached the rough pine casket. Clunk, clunk, clunk . . . I wish I could get that sound out of my head! Mr. Lohmann unscrewed the coffin lid and felt inside.

"Leg's gone. This is Dahlgren all right."

Then Mr. Lohmann and Chris lifted the box onto the wagon. After that we left, Mr. Lohmann's wagon in the lead. Around midnight, we got to William Rowley's farm. Chris helped unload the coffin, and we waited as long as we could for Miss Bet, but he was worried about me being caught, so we started back.

I slipped under my quilt just before Sadie got up to light the fire. Whooee, I'll never forget last night!

Now. How in the world am I going to see Miss Bet?

———◆◆———

APRIL 30, 1864

Dear Lord, please receive the soul of little Joseph Davis. The poor child fell from the balcony railing today and died within minutes. How many times did I tell him, "Don't climb up there!"

Lucy was supposed to be watching Joe when it happened. I was putting Billy down for his nap when she came tearing upstairs to the snuggery where Mr. and Mrs. Davis eat lunch.

"Come quick, Miz Davis, Mistuh Davis," I heard her holler. "Master Joseph done fell from the balcony."

Mrs. Davis let out a scream so loud it bounced off every wall in the mansion. The two of them hurried to the pavement below the balcony and held their son while he died in their arms. I stayed with Billy in case he woke up to his mama's yells and needed me.

Mrs. Davis can't stop crying, and Jeff Davis is crawling with grief. He won't eat or talk to anybody, not even the other children. This evening I dragged myself back up to the nursery, a sack of sorrow heavy on my back. It was hard to believe that just this morning, Joe and I were in there playing games. Now his little five-year-old body is somewhere on a cooling board.

I've kept his paper checkerboard as a memento. He's an angel now—I believe he'd want me to have it.

MAY 7, 1864

10 P.M.

Death and more death, so near. Grant is head of all U.S. armies, and a collar of war chokes Richmond. To the northwest, two days of battle in the great woods of Wilderness. Today's paper says the heat of artillery set the brushy woods on fire, and thousands of wounded Yankees are burning alive.

All day yesterday and today, layers of smoke have muddied the skies. My stomach rolls when I see the unnatural clouds—the ashes of trees and Union men melded as one.

To the south, Butler has moved up the Peninsula, and at this hour he is on Drewry's Bluff, south of the James. Alarm bells rang all day in expectation of his arrival. Stores closed, and streets were empty except for gray-headed old men and barefoot boys. Nelson says they carry nothing with them but cartridge boxes, rusty muskets, and raw courage.

MAY 14, 1864

Awoke to cannon shaking the windows. Sheridan's cavalry is attacking from the north, and Butler's black regiments have taken the port of City Point on the James River. What of Liza's young man? She must feel crazed—if alive, he's only twenty miles away.

The paper says Grant lost twenty-five thousand troops at Wilderness. Still, he presses on to Richmond. The two armies have been fighting at Spotsylvania courthouse for five days.

Quaker made a delivery this morning. He tells me Clara had a visit from Big Belly last night.

"Man can't keep his mouth shut when he's with her," Quaker snickered. "He blabbered about Rebel movements in Spotsylvania. We need to get the details to Grant straight away." I agreed and sent James to the farm wearing his false-soled shoes.

That was early this morning. Since then, Mother, Mary, Caroline, and I have been mindless whirligigs. We dash to the windows, spin down to the garden, then fly to the attic. We search for clues, scan the streets for entering Union troops. It is torment not to know if they are winning!

We try to settle down with meaningless chores . . . polish the silver, arrange flowers. The peonies this year are superb, so Caroline and I cut two dozen. As we carried the baskets of blossoms back to the house, I told her I felt ready to jump out of my skin.

"I'll tell you what," she said. "I already jumped, the day my Liza left for the Confederate White House."

I heard a bevel of pain around her words, and I know I am the cause. I hope she will forgive me one day, for whatever would I do without her and the other servants? Mother and I mingle our hopes, our fears, our prayers with them.

"Nelson, can you tell which are Yankee guns?" I asked last night.

"Yes, missus, them deep ones." Sometimes he encourages and sometimes discourages, and we hang on his words and listen for his faith and hope to strengthen us.

When I open my eyes in the morning, I say to Mary, "What news?" and she never fails me! Most generally, our reliable news is gathered from Negroes, and they certainly show wisdom, discretion, and prudence.

The yearning for deliverance! The uncertain length of our captivity now reckoned by years! How lives the outside world, we wonder?

JUNE 5, 1864

I've been on my knees, praying that Wilson is still alive. Lee reported to Davis this morning: Seven thousand Yankees were killed in two hours at Cold Harbor yesterday. They died and died and died, then thousands more came from behind, fell in line, and died, too.

Cold Harbor is only ten miles to the west. I think one day the bones of these men will rise up, fall together, and march to Richmond for revenge. Miss Bet will be relieved to learn I saw Mr. John's name on the desertion list. Maybe he's safe somewhere.

Terrible hot day. I helped Sadie turn some of Varina's skirts, and we sweated all over them. Poor Varina. The Union blockade keeps supply ships out of Southern harbors, so she hasn't had a new thing to wear in months.

I sneaked a book with engravings out of Jeff's office. Maybe I'll copy a picture to take my mind off the heat. Oh, what's the use? I've probably forgotten how to draw.

For the first time, I am frightened to the point of tears. James found this slipped under the front door. Who are these cowardly White Caps that dare to threaten the Van Lew house?!

I begged James not to tell the others. My only comfort is that Liza may be safer where she is.

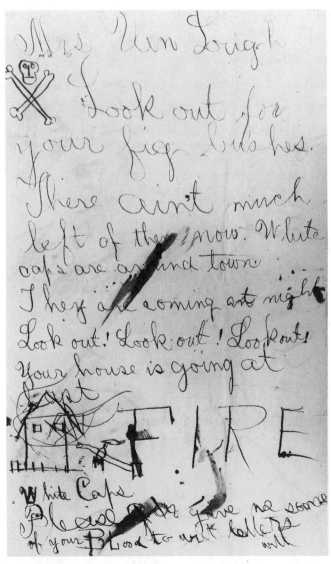

My Dearest Wife,

It is hard to believe I am only a few miles away from your arms. Yet the miles of trenches that stretch around Richmond make you unreachable, as if we're locked in different circles of hell.

I write after two days of battle at New Market Heights, so weary, I barely know my name. My regiment combined with four other colored units to take Fort Harrison on September twenty-ninth and thirtieth. When Rebel guns and cannons poured their fire on us, the men fell in agony. Mercifully, their groans were muffled by the rattle of bayonets, the rain of shot and shell, and the clanking of sabers.

For every Negro soldier left standing, ten or more died. When the bloodbath was over, 543 bodies lay in a spot no bigger than a large vegetable field. By downright determination, the colored troops routed the Rebels out of their stronghold.

My great hope is that our comrades died for a reason. Maybe now the Negro soldier will be respected for his valor in war. Liza, only memories of you have kept me sane.

YOUR AFFECTIONATE HUSBAND,

WILSON

JANUARY 18, 1865

Dear Ellen Bee,

Warning! No time to write in code. I overheard Uncle Jeff talking to an aide this morning. Detectives are assigned to spy on your house. Davis suspects everyone. The spy ring could be broken soon.

Things aren't looking too good for me, either. Aunt Varina called me into the snuggery this afternoon. She said Princess has seen me sifting through Uncle Jeff's trash.

"I'd hate to let you go," she said, "as the children are so fond of you. But if you steal, you will be punished. Do you understand?"

"Yes'm, but I won't be stealing nothing, missus, I declare I won't. It's jes' that sometime I pretend to read them pretty letters Mr. Davis make on the paper, tha's all."

Ellen Bee, I still shake when I think about Wilson at New Market last fall. Now his last letter tells me he is still somewhere outside Richmond, and the regiment is preparing to fight again. I have to talk to you in person!

Dear Ellen Bee,

Let me worry about the spy ring—you have more important work to do. With Grant outside of Petersburg, we daily expect he will take the city soon. Meanwhile, we try to keep food in the house for ourselves and the horse. Zephyr may be one of the few left in Richmond.

Nelson hid him in the smokehouse until James got wind of a Rebel horse raid. We moved him to the study, where he has settled in as a patriot . . . the loyal fellow never neighs or stamps too loudly. Quaker delivers hay in flour sacks so the animal can eat.

Mother bought a cow from Mr. Taylor for fifteen hundred Confederate dollars. The price seems unbelievable, until I remember this is only forty-five dollars in U.S. money. Still, the cow is an extravagance.

I cautioned Mother about spending what few dollars we have left, but she says she cannot face war without milk for her tea and butter for her toast. I kindly reminded her she has only one tin of tea left, and that flour to make bread for toast costs $225 a pound.

Now that Grant's headquarters are nearby at City Point, I've decided the general needs an evening treat—flowers, wrapped in the Richmond morning paper. Nelson sends them by James to the farm, and Bob picks up the relay.

Do you think me foolish, Ellen? After all, Lee's pet chicken travels with him. If Lee can have an egg for breakfast every day, Grant shall have a Rebel paper to read at night.

I hear from Quaker that Sherman will soon take Atlanta and its railroads. He says a Federal victory would calm those in the North who want peace at the price of defeat. He also believes it would help Lincoln in November. If Lincoln loses the election and that coward McClellan wins, the war will end in Confederate victory.

And if the Confederacy becomes a recognized country . . . well, I do not let myself think about what they would do to Ellen Bee. Yet despair is no good. Let us be useful and hopeful instead. Mother and I have much to be thankful for—we have heard from John, and he is safe in the North!

All of us here long to see you, our girl, our wild rose from the garden, sweet and fresh. But you and I must not risk a meeting until Richmond falls. And what a joyous reunion it shall be, here at the mansion with your parents!

◆━◆

JANUARY 20, 1865

Note found in the lion this evening. My Lord, Ellen Bee is now all on her own.

Dear Ellen Bee,

Twelve Union spies arrested today, including six trying to head North. Rebels have already questioned me three times. Pretty roughly, too—I've got poker burns on my back to prove it.

I won't wait for them to visit me again. I'm heading out within the hour. Chris will make deliveries from now on.

It bothers me, leaving Ellen Bee to handle everything alone, but take heart. Now that Atlanta and the port of Wilmington have fallen, the South will dry up from lack of supplies, and famine will spread.

Once Grant takes Petersburg and its railways, the war has to end. If he takes P'burg. The Army of the Potomac has been sitting there for seven months. Must be a lot of card-playing going on.
QUAKER

MARCH 13, 1865
3 P.M.

Dear Ellen Bee,

Uncle Jeff and Aunt Varina had one peppery argument at breakfast. He demanded that she and the children leave Richmond, but she's bitter over the Yankees and doesn't want to give in to them or her husband.

You wouldn't want to hear the nasty things she says about the Federals. Calls them names I've never heard before. I don't know who'll win the Davis war, but soon as there's nothing more I can do, I'm leaving, too. And that's final.

MARCH 26, 1865

Dear Ellen Bee,

Varina and the children are taking the train to Charlotte, North Carolina, tomorrow. I spent the morning packing her silver plate. A few loyal slaves are going with her, like Princess, but hired ones like me have already run off.

I think Princess has pushed a bean of suspicion up her mistress's nose . . . this afternoon, Varina looked at me funny and asked why I'm still here.

So I've got to fly the roost before somebody kills the chicken. I know Mama and Daddy will be afraid for me. Tell them I love them, but I belong with my husband now. If this war ever ends, Wilson and I will come back to visit.

I've never said this before, but I love you, too, Ellen Bee. I'm re-lieved the war is almost over, but I'm glad we got to work together. I believe you've tried to do what's best for me, though sometimes that's been what's best for you.

It's just that you've always wanted me to be your perfect little Negro girl. It was hard to buck that when I was young. Funny thing is, you've made it easy to do it now. I was scared when I went to Philadelphia and scared since I've been here at the White House. So not too much can frighten me anymore.

And here's the other thing. A perfect Negro girl does as she's told. You want me to be a teacher—I want to be a good wife, a mother someday, maybe an artist, or even a writer, like Mr. Freder-ick Douglass.

What if I lived at the mansion? No matter how hard you tried, you'd still give me orders, like you give Mama and Daddy and the rest. You and I, we'd be two teased cats, fighting all the time. I wish I could have said all this to you face-to-face, but it's too late. The sun's going down. Time to slip off, drop this note at Lady's house, and be on my way.

I've got a stash of food in the gunnysack, a strong pair of shoes, and my loyal album. It will always remind me of Ellen Bee. Don't think of me as running away from you. I'm running away to dream my own dreams for a change. Running to find Wilson and my free self.

LOVE,

LIZA

APRIL 1, 1865

Note in the lion this morning—dear Lord, steer my wilful, impossible child away from Petersburg!

> *Big Belly visited last night. Lee is abandoning Richmond-Petersburg defenses. He has only a few soldiers left. Plans to join up with Joe Johnston's troops in N.C.*
>
> *A. P. Hill is ending his medical leave here in Richmond. He's resuming command of his troops east of P'burg. Tell Grant so he can ambush.*
>
> LADY

APRIL 2, 1865

1 A.M.

I write to stay awake, for sleep could mean death by fire—Grant broke through Lee's defenses at Petersburg Sunday morning—A. P. Hill dead—Lee sent a telegram to Davis and said the city must be evacuated—thousands are escaping across Manchester Bridge, their thundering wagons stuffed with boxes and trunks—I daresay the ladies of Richmond have put on weight these last twelve hours—for weeks, they've sewn jewelry into their clothes—pity—great is the desire for tiny waists—

We have been warned that fleeing Rebels plan to set the Van Lew mansion on fire—all day and into the night Caroline and Mary have pumped water into barrels—James and Nelson are hauling them into every room, carting them to the attic and roof—for once, I wish we did not occupy an entire block—the house is too large to protect—

Our attic hideaway has been of use—at midnight I answered a desperate pounding on the door—two prison escapees seeking refuge—they say Rebels have emptied the prisons and are marching the men into the country—these two managed to slip away and come here—

Mother's mind appears to be gone—during the day she rearranged jars of pickles and peach preserves in the pantry—says we must be prepared in case Grant comes to tea—after a cold supper of tinned meat and tinned beans, she fell asleep on Papa's sofa—

I hear Nelson and Caroline still working downstairs—they are frantic about Liza—none of us speak of her possible fate—it is too awful to consider—hundreds of Rebel soldiers are deserting every day—starvation has turned some into animals. Is A. T. one of them—or even alive—I think not—an emptiness in my heart tells me he is gone forever—I must pull myself from this chair and go down, tell the servants to get some sl———

———◆◆———

APRIL 3, 1865

9 A.M.

The city of my birth is in flames! I should record these fateful moments, for who knows what will happen to me by the end of this day? When dawn exploded at 4:30, I tumbled from the chair and shrieked. As windows shattered, shards of glass flew across the room. Certain the hour of my death was at hand, I prayed until good dear Mary dashed upstairs and helped me to my feet.

"Mother . . . ?" I asked, sure that she was in flames.

"Mrs. Van Lew, she fine. Still half asleep and mumbling something about fixing her hair for General Grant."

"Nelson . . . Caroline . . . your James?"

"They all right, too. Nelson says the explosion is the Confederate Navy, blowing up its own warships at Rockett's Landing."

Can this be less than five hours ago? Chaos keeps a devilish slow time. The explosions seem never to stop—tobacco warehouses, arsenals—each boom rattles the house harder than the last. We haven't lost our chimneys yet, thank God.

Nelson and James went out as the sun rose. They returned in an hour, and we all met them in the front hall, eager for news. They say a breeze is spreading fire throughout the business section.

"Most of the buildings are smoking shells," James reported. "Single walls and chimneys, standing like wounded soldiers too tired to fall."

"But we're delivered!" Nelson announced. "Union troops entered the city at seven-twenty. I know for sure, 'cause when I saw that blue line marching double-time up Main Street, I looked at my pocket watch. If Liza comes home, I want to tell her everything exactly like it happened."

"What you mean, if?" Caroline said. She wiped her eyes on her sleeve. "She'll be back. And when she is, she'll get a good shaking. Running off like that, not even saying good-bye."

"Anyway," James said, "crowds of colored citizens were singing, hugging the men's horses, kissing the soliders' legs! Even the Rebels look relieved, though a few are still waving Confederate flags. They won't get away with that for long."

Nelson turned to Caroline. "You know the Forrester boy?"

"Narcissa's son? That light-skinned one live over on College Street?"

"Well, he's been working at the Capitol building all through the war. Soon as the Yankees got to the Capitol, Richard Forrester went to the top floor and hung the Stars and Stripes from the pole. Told me he saved it from the trash pile the day Fort Sumter fell. He's been hiding it under his mattress ever since."

Mother's frail voice interrupted the rejoicing. "Where is our flag, Bet? The one Butler sent us?"

I retrieved the flag from under a chaise in the study and carefully unfolded it for all to see. Nelson hung it, a glorious twenty by nine feet, from the front porch.

As he stuck it in the pole, an angry mob jumped the iron fence and crowded into the yard. I made him go inside and addressed the crowd myself.

"Lower this flag," I called out, "or hurt one bit of my house, and I'll see that General Butler pays you back in kind . . . every one of you!"

Their threats continued, but several faces in the throng were familiar. I pointed to them. "I know you . . . and you!" Then I turned and went in, leaving them to their insults. A few are out there still, their voices growing hoarse.

Never mind, I have more important matters to attend to. For four years I have been a blackmailer and a liar. What difference does it make if I become a thief? I know it is foolish, now that people realize Crazy Bet is not so crazy after all. Caroline would say don't go troubling trouble, but I am going out in the smoky city to find what I can.

There may be documents in the Capitol ruins—reports that would incriminate Ellen Bee. Or what if Liza lost her album somewhere and a Rebel has it now? Southern vengeance would ruin her chance for happiness in this city. I must do all I can to make Richmond a safe haven for my girl when she comes back.

And she will come back. Liza thinks I tried to run her life, though, heavens above, what seems like taking charge to her feels like work and worry to me! Perhaps I spoiled her, did too much for her, but it was only out of love.

She is a smart girl—when I find her, I will explain myself. She will understand. She has to. Because she *must* come home. Home to her parents, this house, and me. I may not love her the most, but I *do* love her the best.

Epilogue

Now, Polly, would you like to know what became of Ellen Bee? A few sundry scraps in the back of the album help tell the story. First, this drawing of the Confederate White House that I clipped from the paper.

Federal troops occupied it for five years, then it became a school. Three years ago, in 1896, Southern ladies opened it as a Confederate Museum. I doubt they'd let a Negro girl in, but if you visit, you'll find paintings and war relics and dead memories. You won't find anything about Ellen Bee.

Looking at the place now, it's hard to believe I ever worked there as a spy. Daddy always said you don't know what you can do until you have to, and he was right. But thank goodness I took the chance. General Grant said there were times when the only intelligence coming out of Richmond was from Bet Van Lew. What he doesn't know is that it came from Ellen Bee.

Here's a picture of the fall of Richmond. Miss Bet found it in a New York newspaper and sent it to me. After the city fell, Lee and his troops tried to make it to North Carolina, but Grant cut him off near Appomattox Courthouse. The few Rebel soldiers left were outnumbered, broken-down, and starving. To their credit, they would have kept fighting if their general had given the word. Instead, he surrendered on April 9, 1865.

President Lincoln was assassinated on April 14, and in May, old Jeff Davis was captured and put in jail. With that, the Confederacy was dead and the war was over.

I did find my Wilson, wounded but still alive in a hospital

near Fort Hamilton. For years, we said prayers of thanks that he wasn't captured. He could have ended up like these prisoners at Belle Isle.

After the war, Wilson and I taught at the Benjamin Butler

 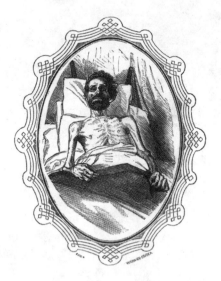

School at Fort Monroe. We visited Miss Bet a few times, but it was never easy. Just like I thought, we always argued. Then Mama died, and Daddy went two weeks later. For months all I did was cry, so we moved on up North.

Part of me hated to leave Old Virginia, and part of me still loves the South. But the burned-out city was too desolate, and we never really felt safe there. Besides, we had Wilson's folks to think about. We worried what people would do if they found out about the Liza half of Ellen Bee.

Richmonders did find out what Miss Bet had done, and they haven't spoken to her since. Mr. John came home and re-opened the hardware stores after the war. But no one would buy from a Van Lew, so the stores closed, and he and his family moved in with Miss Bet. She kept one of the last receipts, I guess to remind herself of better days.

Miss Bet's mother died in 1870, and do you know what?

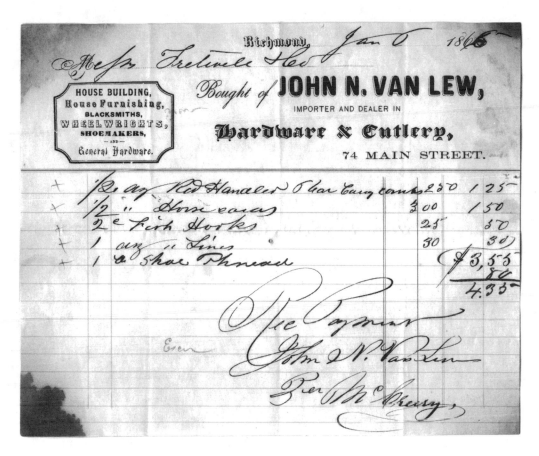

People called it a "nigger funeral." Miss Bet couldn't even find enough pallbearers to carry the casket. So much for the Christians at St. John's. She's even given up visits to White Sulphur Springs—the hotel won't rent her a room.

The children have been the worst. I guess her "Crazy Bet" reputation hung on, because they think she's a witch and they scream "Yankee" under her windows. She tries to be nice and had an ice-cream party for them one time. But nothing helps, so she's started screaming back, "I'm not a Yankee!" And she isn't. She's as Southern as grits and gravy. That's why she suffers the torment and never moves away.

Some things turned out all right, at least for a while. After the war, General Grant was elected president of the United States. To reward Miss Bet for her work, he made her postmistress of

Richmond. She did a fine job for eight years, though nobody in town would admit it. Pretty strict with the workers . . . even fired a group of them who didn't like working for a woman.

Quaker went back to Richmond and still lives there. He and some of his spy friends used to celebrate the anniversary of A. P. Hill's death at the foot of Hill's statue. I guess they're too old for that now, but from what I hear, he's still full of spit.

Clara Coleman made out well. At age forty she married a man with money, and together they started a successful department store. I'll always be grateful to Lady for taking Wilson and me in. She knew more about being a lady than some of those "first family of Virginia" types.

John died in 1895, so now Miss Bet rolls around in that big old house with only her niece, Eliza, Mr. A. T.'s old watch, and forty cats to keep her company. She and the niece fight a lot, which doesn't surprise me one bit. Miss Bet says Eliza cleans the house too much. Eliza thinks Miss Bet complains a lot.

Especially about property taxes. Miss Bet pays them every year, but sends the same letter every time. She says it's taxation without representation, since women don't get to vote. That's just like her!

Here's a photograph Miss Bet sent me a while back. She's a tiny woman, but believe me, she's stronger than she looks, and nobody knows that like I do.

Miss Bet is eighty-one now, and though her penmanship is shaky, we still write. Still disagree, too. But we know that during the war years we were somebody special. A young black woman, an older white one . . . together we made history. So now you know who Ellen Bee was, Polly. She was a hero. And now that you have her scrapbook, maybe one day someone else will know it, too.

LOVE,

AUNT LIZA

About the Text

The real Elizabeth Van Lew (1818–1900) kept a scrapbook for over forty years and a diary that totaled seven hundred pages. Only four hundred pages of the diary survive. Mary Elizabeth Bowser (1846?–?) may have kept an album that contained references to a man named Davis. Her great-niece by marriage believes she accidentally threw it away sometime in the 1950s.

As we wrote *Dear Ellen Bee*, we tried to imagine what the missing papers might have revealed about these two courageous women and their relationship. *Dear Ellen Bee*, then, is a fictional story, but it is based on real characters and events inspired by existing historical documents.

These include Van Lew's diary and scrapbook and a memoir dictated by Quaker. Quaker's real name was Thomas McNiven (1835–1904). He kept a detailed diary during the Civil War, but the executor of his estate destroyed it in 1906. Before Quaker died, he dictated his memories to his oldest daughter, who retold them to her grandson, Robert Waitt, in 1952. Waitt conducted further research on Bowser and Van Lew. We based the year of Bowser's birth and marriage on his research findings.

Bowser's contributions to the Union victory in the Civil War are noted in two places outside Virginia. In 1977, a tree was planted in her honor at a military cemetery in the Bronx, New York. On June 30, 1995, she was posthumously inducted into the U.S. Army's Military Intelligence Corps Hall of Fame at Fort Huachuca, Arizona.

In 1994, the Virginia Business and Professional Women's Foundation and the Virginia Foundation for the Humanities and Public Policy mounted a plaque to honor Mary Elizabeth Bowser. The plaque is in the lobby of a school erected on the former site of Elizabeth Van Lew's mansion. It is the only public memorial to Bowser in Virginia.

The plaque reads: FREED SLAVE OF THE VAN LEW FAMILY AND INDISPENS-

ABLE PARTNER TO ELIZABETH VAN LEW IN HER PRO-UNION ESPIONAGE WORK, SHE WORKED AT THE CONFEDERATE WHITE HOUSE GATHERING AND PASSING ON MILITARY INTELLIGENCE TO THE UNION THROUGH VAN LEW TO GENERAL GRANT.

Elizabeth Van Lew is buried in the family plot in Shochoe Cemetery, Richmond, Virginia. On the day she was buried, Quaker stayed by the grave for hours after her family left. "It was like I had lost my mother," he remembered. Her grave is marked by a two-feet-high, four-feet-long slab of gray stone. Erected by friends in Massachusetts, the plaque on the stone reads:

> *ELIZABETH VAN LEW   1818–1900*
> *She risked everything that is dear to man—friends, fortune, comfort, health, life itself, all for the one absorbing desire of her heart, that slavery be abolished and the Union be preserved.*

The following text is adapted from Elizabeth Van Lew's diary: p. 84, Confederate women's comments on Yankees; p. 123, description of famine in Richmond; p. 136, comments on servants and the war; p. 148, responses to the mob. For complete text of Van Lew's diary, see *A Yankee Spy in Richmond: The Civil War Diary of "Crazy Bet" Van Lew*, edited by David Ryan (Mechanicsburg, PA: Stackpole Books, 1996).

About the the Illustrations

Illustrations in *Dear Ellen Bee* were inspired by a variety of nineteenth-century Southern scrapbooks, including the album kept by Elizabeth Van Lew. Girls and women stored their dearest items in scrapbooks: letters, copied poems, clippings, ribbons, flowers, leaves, signatures, lists of books, drawings, calling cards, greeting cards, jokes, medals, badges, envelopes, photos, stamps, telegrams, even money. Albums held secret thoughts, too. When paper was unavailable during the Civil War, southern girls used blank scrapbook pages for their journal entries.

The illustration at the top of Liza's scrapbook pages is taken from a commercially-printed nineteenth-century scrapbook entitled "Album." The hand-drawn vine at the top of Miss Bet's pages is from a nineteenth-century scrapbook kept by a young Virginia woman. The presentation scroll and flourishes are from a collection of nineteenth-century Southern scrapbooks provided by Heartwood Used and Rare Books, Charlottesville, Virginia.

p. 2: Liza's freedom paper based on Harriet Bolling's certificate of freedom, Petersburg, Virginia, 1851. Carter G. Woodson Collection, Manuscript Division. (2-2) Library of Congress, Washington, D.C.

p. 5: Liza's train ticket based on an original from the collection of Calvin Otto. The Rebus says, "Put this in your hat or cap and keep your seat and not be running from car to car and you'll ride safe and not be flipped."

p. 34: Frederick Douglass broadside from the Library Company of Philadelphia, Philadelphia, Pennsylvania.

p. 42: "Address of John Brown . . . Sentence of Death; For his heroic attempt at Harpers Ferry . . ." Boston: C. C. Mead. Broadside, Rare Book and Special Collections Division (3-6), Library of Congress, Washington, D.C.

p. 45: Sketch of wedding dress by Dennis Winston, Richmond, Virginia.

p. 56: "Proclamation by the Governor of Virginia." *The Daily Richmond*

Enquirer—Semi-Weekly Edition. Tuesday Morning, April 18, 1861, number 103, pg. 2. ACC # 99-0220, the Library of Virginia, Richmond, Virginia.

p. 64: "News by Telegraph." *The Daily Richmond Enquirer.* Monday Morning, July 22, 1861, number 147, p. 3. ACC #99-0226, the Library of Virginia, Richmond, Virginia.

p. 81: "Attention Citizens!" broadside from Elizabeth Van Lew's scrapbook, Virginia Historical Society, Richmond, Virginia.

p. 86–87: Map of Libby Prison from *Illustrated Guide to Richmond, The Confederate Capital with A Facsimile Reprint of the City Intelligencer of 1862.* (Richmond, VA: The Confederate Museum, 1960).

p. 92: "Come and Join Us Brothers" recruitment poster from the Chicago Historical Society, Chicago, Illinois.

p. 102: Code adapted from the original in the Van Lew Papers, Special Collections, New York Public Library.

p. 102: Sketch of peach pit pin by Dennis Winston.

p. 113: Photograph of amputation from the National Archives, Washington, D.C.

p. 118: Libby Prison playbill from the Van Lew Papers, College of William and Mary, Williamsburg, Virginia.

p. 134: "The War of the Disunited States" checkerboard from the collection of Calvin Otto.

p. 138: Photograph of White Caps hate note from the Van Lew Papers, Special Collections, New York Public Library.

p. 150–51: Drawing of Confederate White House and the fall of Richmond from *Illustrated Guide to Richmond, The Confederate Capital with A Facsimile Reprint of the City Intelligencer of 1862.* (Richmond, Virginia: The Confederate Museum, 1960).

p. 155: Photograph of Elizabeth Van Lew from the Valentine Museum, Richmond, Virginia. There is no known photograph of Mary Elizabeth Bowser.

Acknowledgments

I am most grateful to Mary E. Lyons for inviting me to be her coauthor. She has been an outstanding mentor and model for me as a neophyte fiction writer. Gratitude is also extended posthumously to Robert Waitt, colleague and friend, who so generously shared his grandfather's oral history and allowed me to hold the famed peach pit pin; to McEva Bowser, great-niece-in-law of Mary Elizabeth Bowser, who granted an interview and provided several valuable secondary sources regarding public monuments; to Teresa Roane, at the Valentine Museum, who piled nineteenth-century scrapbooks chin-high on a table and invited me to spend hours looking through them; to Audrey Johnson, at the Library of Virginia, for locating and photographing the 1861 newspaper articles; to the staff of the Library Company of Philadelphia for their assistance in unearthing details on the Quaker schools for Negroes in Philadelphia, and for access to the John Brown papers; to Mr. Robert E. L. Krick, Historian, Richmond National Battlefield Park, for providing a copy of the J. J. Scroggs' papers and several secondary sources pertaining to the Battle of New Market Heights; and to the staff at the Casemate Museum, Fort Monroe, Virginia, who provided access to the Benjamin Butler papers.

My sincerest thanks are extended to my mother, Missouri Walthall Miller, who, through normal conversation, unwittingly supplied many of the "fresh" phrases used in the text; to my husband, Willis, for his critical listening ear; to my friend, Audrey V. Jones, who spent hours in the National Archives researching Wilson Bowser's military records; to my artist friend, Dennis R. Winston, who rendered sketches for the book on very short notice; to my friend and former supervisor, Dr. Delores Z. Pretlow, who put me in touch with McEva Bowser; and to Shatara Mayfield, an eighth-grade student at Thompson Middle School, who read each version of the text with great enthusiasm and insight.   —M. B.

A number of friends and colleagues offered assistance while I worked on *Dear Ellen Bee*. The contributions of the following people are too many to list here, but y'all know what y'all did:

Janet Anderson; Joy Antrim; Angela and Dick Brown; Catherine Clinton; Arthur Collier; Roberta Culbertson; Irene, Franny, and Jocelyn, from the Village School; Rita Koman; Jon Lanman; Joe Lyons; Calvin and Patricia Otto; Bill Reiss; Sheilah Scott; Jane Smith; Leni Sorensen; Amelia Thompson-Deveaux; Shirley Washington; Lauren Winner; Ann York.

I thank my mother and posthumously my father for their marvelous Southern accents and phrases. Both flavor the voices of characters in *Dear Ellen Bee*. Special thanks to my coauthor, Muriel Branch, with whom I shared egg salad sandwiches (no pickles!), the longest and most delicious laugh of my life, and many trustful talks about slavery and race relations. Finally, thanks to my husband, Paul Collinge, for always doing the taxes.

—M.L.

The authors are grateful to the Virginia Foundation for the Humanities and Public Policy, Charlottesville, Virginia, for its commitment to funding scholarship in the areas of women's history, cultural diversity, and children's literature. Our collaborative fellowship at the Virginia Center for the Humanities allowed us to complete *Dear Ellen Bee* in the spring of 1999.